Dear Beverly,
I hope you find
inspiration in these pages.
Thank you for your support.

Warm Regards
Kirk Martin
07-13-02

W9-AZO-337

SHADE

OF

THE

MAPLE

Kirk Martin

———————————

SHADE

OF

THE

MAPLE

Cantwell-Hamilton Press

This book is a work of fiction. Names, characters, places and incidents are the product of the author's imagination or are used fictitiously. Any resemblance to actual events, locales, or persons, living or dead, is coincidental.

Copyright © 2002 by Kirk L. Martin
All rights reserved.

Please visit us on the web
www.shadeofthemaple.com

Cantwell-Hamilton Press, LLC
1589 Skeet Club Road, Suite 102, Box 351
High Point, North Carolina 27265

ISBN 0-9716145-0-4

Library of Congress Control Number: 2001119564

Cover design by Julie Staton
Digital artist, Steve Koger

Printed in the United States of America
10 9 8 7 6 5 4 3 2 1

to my angel

Prologue

A BRISK autumn breeze accompanied the broken man like an old friend as he ambled over the familiar sidewalk. His worn feet knew every crack and rift splitting the unforgiving cement squares he had greeted for the past fifty years. And the sidewalk knew him intimately. Some days, it mourned the lumbering gait of a grieving man, tasting the bitter drops of his tears. Others, it reveled in the triumphal float of a man ignited by a larger purpose. This path could tell the story of a man who lived a life inside his own mind, longing for a time that always seemed beyond his grasp.

A young couple, swinging hands and sharing an ice cream cone, waltzed past him, unaware that he understood the feeling. To them, he was a stranger's forgotten grandfather, a faceless man without a story. Ah, he thought, the blissful foolishness of adolescent love. Oblivious to everything except themselves, disregarding reason, savoring ice cream on a chilly day. Unsure if they are so much in love with each other as they are with the delirium of love itself. A prayer whispered under his breath. Let them know a consuming love forged by trial as well. Their giggling trailed away into the crackling of leaves beneath his feet.

Stepping into the small market, he unzipped his jacket and roamed the narrow aisles, carefully picking necessities from the shelves. He exchanged a smile and wishes for a pleasant evening with the shopkeeper before bundling up and heading home.

The faint smell of smoke drifting from distant chimneys heralded the arrival of fall together with its first tastes of winter, stirring thoughts from the carefree days of his youth. He remembered waking to bright autumn mornings. A northeasterly chill replaced the fire of summer, beckoning for sweatshirts and football games on lawns dappled with vivid reds and oranges and golds. Each snapping gust unleashing an avalanche of leaves. The discomfort of callused hands and sore back—from dragging a rake across the yard—quickly forgotten in the joy of countless leaps into scattered piles. Nothing could be better than New England in autumn, the allure of Thanksgiving and Christmas in the air. The sun in its unselfish glory would gradually yield to the reign of the forbidding moon as days shortened, playtime outdoors measured in minutes.

Boisterous shrieks in the darkening sky conjured images of young boys playing football. Dingy sweatshirts sullied by dirt and grass pressed into creases, sweat beading on foreheads, faces flush with the intensity of competition buffered by the resiliency of friendship.

As the final glow of amber surrendered to dusk, the town retreated into the warmth of their homes, the yellow din glowing through frosted windowpanes. The dry, piercing night air muted his nostrils, the only discernable scent the familiar smoke from innumerable fireplaces. He pictured logs carefully laid over blackened grates, the first crackles of splintered kindling delighting children, the emanating warmth drawing families together.

Finally reaching home, he lumbered up the wide plank steps, glancing up at stars forming out of darkness before turning the knob. He moved through the black hallway to the kitchen and set the groceries on wooden countertops. Into the worn cupboards cans of soup and vegetables took their places as if they knew where they belonged. The refrigerator welcomed the milk, eggs and juice.

He retired to his den, the candle's soft glimmer lighting the creased paper beneath his hands, throwing flickering shadows against the wall. After a short time, he cupped his hand around the candle and blew. He trod down the narrow hallway, opened the door to the back porch, and fell into the comfort of his rocking chair. The moon cast its silvery glow upon the hushed countryside, silence broken only by the constant creaking of the empty chair beside him. As he had over the course of a lifetime, he slipped into another world and relived a story that echoed through his soul day after day, a story shaped by Vermont and a young woman—until shaken by a profound thought:

He had spent his life living for the promise of the future. Now he was grasping for a past beyond his reach.

Chapter 1

SLUMPED OVER in bed, clutching rumpled flannel sheets and blankets bundled at her waist, Anna bit her lip, fighting to silence troubled gasps. She glanced at her husband. His eyes were closed, oblivious to her grimace, unaware of her struggle. The words blurred as the pages that held her gaze revealed a reality beyond the world of fiction. The novel ceased to be inhabited by invented characters. There was something oddly familiar about this couple. She knew them.

Kelli awoke in the middle of the night, thirsty for water. A simple drawing hung from the bathroom mirror. She peeled the tape, examining the picture. Glittering stars scattered about a large yellow sun drawn with a heavy crayon—its rays protruding in uneven lengths—rested above a sliver of moon illuminating a night sky.

She smiled. In a small woven basket on the vanity, an envelope sat propped against matching hand towels. Kelli opened the note.

You are the sun, the moon and the stars all shining together at the same time.

You are the sun that warms me by day, the moon that comforts me at night and the bright light that guides my way.

Without you, I would be lost.

In case you haven't noticed, the big oaf lying next to you in bed is madly in love with you. Now will you please come and snuggle with me?

Awaiting your touch,
Justin

Anna closed the book and stared at it mystically before placing it on the nightstand. She loved David, she told herself, as she kissed him softly on the cheek goodnight. He's a good man. She reached up and with a click, darkness became her cover. Anna stared blankly at familiar shadows, weeping inside. Tomorrow is a new day, she thought.

The Adirondacks stood proudly silhouetted against a translucent blue haze, its rugged contours and four thousand foot peaks reflecting first light. Birds flitted in bursts between perches on fence posts and rooftops, chirping feverishly as if revealing urgent news. David stood in the driveway wearing ragged shorts and tee shirt, captive to his talkative neighbor. He restlessly twirled his much-awaited Sunday morning paper round and round, drops of dew leaping from the plastic wrap. Two squealing girls darted between, around and into the men, competing for their father's attention. Their mother marched outside, crouching to retrieve the blue pinwheel bows from the grass and fix them just so. She tugged and brushed their frumpled dresses, then scooted them toward the minivan. The distant clanging of church bells freed David.

Anna stretched and yawned, enjoying the view and the warm breeze through the open bedroom window. Local weathermen were no doubt in their glory, taking credit for a seventy-five degree day—not bad for Burlington, Vermont in late September. These same forecasters would soon be apologizing nightly for the six-month reign of frigid air and interminable snow.

Sunlight splashed into the airy master bedroom as Anna tucked sheets and fluffed pillows. The garnet and sage comforter added life to a room whose walls wore a stark white coat, like most in this contemporary colonial. David and Anna bought the new home in June, on their fourth wedding anniversary, and it still mirrored the builder's sallow personality. Anna steadily made progress, accenting each room, including a stenciled border in this one. There were two other bedrooms to decorate, not to mention three bathrooms and the downstairs living areas.

Anna grabbed the empty glass on the nightstand and walked downstairs, stopping to straighten the disheveled throw rug in the foyer and admire the chair rail she had added in the formal dining room. Light flooded through large kitchen windows. David hid behind the newspaper, a smattering of piles—read, throw out, catalogs and coupons—concealing an oak table.

"Good morning, David."

"Hey, honey," a voice called from behind the newspaper.

"Where's *Travel?*"

"Think it's over there," David replied, blindly motioning toward the *throw out* pile. Anna always read her favorite section first.

6

"Susan mentioned a feature today on fall getaways in New England and Canada. I thought it would be fun to do one weekend."

"Uh huh. Sounds good."

"We could drive to New Hampshire on a Friday night and stay in a little Bed-and-Breakfast. You know, make a weekend of it. What about Bar Harbor? The lighthouses and whale-watching tours are..."

"Have you noticed all the construction up off 89? Apparently new businesses are bringing in lots of jobs."

Anna scanned the pages. "What about Quebec? We could see the snow geese migrating from the Arctic and magnificent apple orchards. They have some special packages..."

"I don't know. Haven't really thought about it, honey." David tossed the paper aside, rose from the table and kissed Anna on the forehead. "Hey, are you ready for breakfast?"

"Yeah. Want some help?"

"I'll get it. Scrambled eggs and bacon okay?"

"That's great. Why don't I fix the bacon while you get the eggs?" Anna offered.

"No. That's okay," David said, opening the refrigerator. "I was thinking about inviting Ron over this afternoon. Patriots are playing the Giants—should be a good game."

"Oh, I was hoping we could spend time outside together since it's warm. Maybe plant shrubs and spring bulbs, straighten up before it turns cold."

"I guess I could cut the grass one more time. I'll tell Ron we'll have to catch the game next week."

The garage door opened and David backed out of the driveway, waving to neighbors joining in the Sunday

7

morning stampede to church. David and Anna Collins lived in Colchester, a sprawling suburb north of Burlington. Carved from farmland, the recently developed subdivision boasted sixty-five homes, mainly variations of two-story colonials, bunched together on three-quarter acre lots. A few trees remained on their property, but not enough to offer either shade or privacy. As they drove south, Anna thought about her plans to border the back yard with fast-growing Leyland cypress trees, which would proudly display coming snows.

They attended an old church in Burlington's historic district. Many buildings dated to the city's founding in the 1770's. With a gentle agricultural landscape punctuated by dairy farms, Burlington rested on the shores of Lake Champlain in a picturesque valley between the Adirondack Mountains to the west and Green Mountains eastward. Even at this early hour, the sparkling waters of the lake were swathed in a bountiful rainbow of sails, vibrant as blue sky draped with hot air balloons. Boaters were reveling in this final gift of nature. Anna sat through church guiltily distracted by thoughts of gardening.

The cool dirt felt like silk treasure pouring through her fingers. Anna derived satisfaction from transforming a barren plot into a bed bursting with colorful flowers and plants. She used her gift for creating to build a thriving business downtown. Her shop had flourished into a marketplace mainstay, selling crafts, gifts and keepsakes fashioned with her own hands.

Earlier in the summer, she planted daisies, sunflowers, baby's breath and a variety of ornamentals, partly for use in her shop. Hollies spotted the front and back yards. The jewel red berries would provide food for her birds and a breathtaking contrast against the first snow.

Anna's knees lived in the dirt hour after hour, planting a mix of shrubs and bulbs—daffodils, hyacinth, and tulips—that would remain dormant during the long Vermont winter and bloom the following spring.

By mid-afternoon, the reverberating drone of lawnmowers had been replaced by a symphony of children shrieking, giggling and crying. It reminded Anna of something her eldest brother said—her envy would disappear when it was *her* child screaming for attention. The neighbors were likely craving a peaceful afternoon.

"The grass is done and I cleaned out the garage," David said, arching his back. "I'm going in."

"Is your back sore?" Anna asked.

"A little bit, no big deal," David replied, still stretching.

"How about a backrub later on?"

"Sounds fine."

Anna stepped back to examine her efforts, head tilted, contemplating. "What do you think about my flower bed?"

"Looks great," David replied, walking away.

"Do you think the combinations are good? I wonder if I need to add some color or maybe…"

"I don't know, Anna. This is your thing. I told you I think it looks really good."

Anna breathed a heavy sigh as David wandered away. She remained silent, instead turning to her work. The flowerbed needed definition. Her knees hit the dirt. She sculpted the soil, creating a border with small plants. Rising to her feet, Anna stared at the bed again, content with her work.

But troubled by David's indifference.

Anna persisted outside, unwilling to relinquish this day to colder ones following, until the sun faded against a cloudless sky. She loaded the red wheelbarrow with a torn bag of topsoil, gardening tools and a tangle of weeds. She trudged to the cedar shed, put everything in its place and returned for a final survey of her work.

The aroma of steaks and burgers on neighbors' grills permeated the subdivision. The flavor drifted through the air, so inviting she could taste the steak. Anna considered sauntering to the far side of her yard to prompt an invitation from friends. The image of a family cookout kindled vivid childhood memories.

It wasn't really the food. It was the whole experience. Dirty and exhausted from playing under the scorching sun all day. Resting at the foot of a magnificent oak, gazing up through limbs and leaves at puffy evening clouds. Flames shooting from the grill. Her father waiting patiently for the black coals to heat to an ashen white. Ketchup and mustard and buns and paper plates crowding the picnic table. Inviting her best friend to stay, her parents forgetting to make them wash up before dinner. Birds singing and dogs barking and everyone laughing. Shooing away flies, scratching arms itchy from bug bites, gobbling down chips and soda and hot dogs with black stripes. And spying the bag of marshmallows. After you finish your meal, Anna. Yes, you may be excused. Frolicking and giggling with her girlfriend until God painted the sky red and orange and purple. Her father calling. Time to roast marshmallows. Leaning over the coals, a blast of heat like a hair dryer blowing in her face. Impatiently reaching the stick too close to the embers, huffing and puffing to extinguish the blazing marshmallow. Giving the burned ones to Mom. Finally feeling the crunchy coating warm her mouth, the sticky goo inside stretching from the stick like elastic. Licking her fingers and lips, snacking until her stomach ached.

The neighbor's invitation was not forthcoming. Reminiscing would suffice for the night.

Chapter 2

ANNA COLLINS had been shaped in large measure by her upbringing in a quaint hamlet in central Vermont. Brandon was happily nestled against the magnificent backdrop of the Green Mountains, Vermont's portion of the Appalachian Mountain Range. Stately old homes lined broad avenues and the Neshobe River flowed between two village greens. White church steeples spiraled brilliantly into deep blue heavens, clothed in the boundless kaleidoscope of autumn. Fiery maples joined with majestic dark spruces to surround the town, forming a protective barrier from the outside world. The community that molded Anna was self-sustaining. Abundant dairy farms, apple orchards and maple sap afforded a sound economic foundation. Old-fashioned virtues of hard work, integrity and responsibility—for yourself and others—remained as integral to life in Brandon as baseball and Coca-Cola to other towns. These values were not preached, just practiced in a way that everyone understood—and the reason Brandon thrived all the same during economic boom or downturn.

Anna's grandparents built a small hardware store in Brandon after the Great Depression. The store sold the wares of local craftsmen, but broadened its product lines to meet the needs of a growing town, not to mention smaller villages beyond. Matthews' Mercantile was not only the center of her family's life—it became the heart of the community. The two were inextricably linked. Her grandparents shared a simple vision. Every person who walked through the doors should leave feeling better about himself than when he entered. Over time, legends spread about a man who placed bags of groceries, under cover of night, outside the homes of families in need. The man in all the stories was her grandfather. No one knew for certain and no one ever asked. But even a child could hear the truth in the respectful tone with which townspeople greeted her family.

By the time Anna's grandfather passed away and her father took over, Matthews' Mercantile sold everything from hinges and hardware to bubble gum and grocery items. An authentic old General Store. And a genuine family business.

Anna and her two older brothers grew up in the store. Her fondest memories sprang from the Mercantile. Leaping off wooden steps to the dusty, but welcoming ground below on hot afternoons. Steps that seemed a mile high to a toddler and her friends. Cuddling in Grandma's lap, a refreshing breeze swaying an old pine swing on the front porch. Listening to grown-ups share gracious words with neighbors and strangers alike. Giggling while hiding from boys behind crates of soda bottles. The reassurance of her mother's touch, one hand warm on Anna's shoulder and the other stroking her hair while talking to a customer.

The anticipation of seeing her father after school. She would burst out the schoolhouse doors, tear across open fields and wooded paths until she spotted the familiar pitched roof of the Mercantile rising above small trees. From there, she would scamper across the narrow footbridge, up the stairs, through the door and into her father's arms. Even now,

Anna could hear the precise pitch and clang of the bells that danced against the glass. Her father told her the bells played a different song when his little girl came through the door. And like a grown child whose willingness to believe in Santa defies common sense, Anna always believed her father's claim and reveled in being his "Annabell". Until, of course, at age twelve she proclaimed herself a *woman* and beyond such a childish nickname.

The same security that fostered Anna's growing independence gave her the confidence to challenge an unspoken tenet governing decisions about the future: Anna and her brothers would continue in the family business. But she inherited a curiosity not common to her brothers. Though Anna's father followed closely in her grandfather's footsteps, he craved the occasional stray path. When she was young, her father placed her atop crates stacked high in the backroom, legs dangling, where she watched him work. Shouts of instructions from her grandfather bellowed through the store, to which her father nodded and replied dutifully. But not without glancing up at her with a wink and knowing smile. Even as a child, Anna understood the glimmer of independence in his eyes.

When opportunities for travel arose—to attend trade shows or purchase supplies—her father could not wait to embark on his adventure. It remained a memory Anna and her brothers recalled with fondness—the still night interrupted by whispers from their parents' bedroom, the creaking hallway, a kiss on the forehead, the front door shutting and the car rumbling away. Days later, the door swung open and the colossal man would stride through. Suitcases clunked to the floor, little arms and legs climbed the giant like schoolchildren on a jungle gym. He somehow managed a kiss for their mom through the clamor. His eyes were alive with tales of magical cities—towering skyscrapers, hordes of people cramming huge buses and underground trains, streets alive with the commotion of cabs honking, pigeons flapping and lights flashing. Anna wanted to go there, too.

Books temporarily satisfied her quest for exploration. She was a pioneer, traversing the frontier by covered wagon with Laura Ingalls. She was a mischievous red-haired orphan, finding trouble at every turn on picturesque Prince Edward Island with Anne of Green Gables. She was absorbed into the New England countryside by Robert Frost. It was no surprise when, in her junior year at Brandon High, Anna announced her decision to strike out on her own after graduation. No, I don't have a plan. Yes, I know we can't afford college. Her mother objected. Her father caught the glimmer.

Anna said goodbye to her family. Two girlfriends were moving to Middlebury after their senior year and needed a roommate. She settled into her first apartment, near Canterbury College, away from her parents' home, but only by an hour. She secured a full-time job at the college bookstore. It was perfect. Surrounded by books, in the midst of campus activity, an environment of learning and adventure. Though textbooks appeared dry and encyclopedic, the worlds of new information fascinated Anna.

College boys also intrigued her. At first. She was pleasantly surprised by the overwhelming interest from the young men she met at the bookstore—Brandon had offered limited opportunities. But the excitement wore off quickly. They were either boring, immature or conceited. One was different. Evan Forrester. Her first real love. First loves never worked out, did they? Anna eventually moved to

Burlington, where she met David. A little staid, but kind, dependable and handsome. She had no doubt he would be a faithful husband and loving father. He proposed on bended knee with roses in one hand, ring in the other. Her family welcomed him with open arms. After graduating from the University of Vermont, David accepted an offer with a top accounting firm in Burlington. Anna scouted the perfect location for a downtown gift shop, where she could carry on the spirit of her family's tradition.

Dried flowers, ribbons, bows, angel wings and countless odds and ends lay strewn about the old shaker farm table waiting patiently to be brought to life. Anna had transformed a cold, dingy warehouse into a cozy workroom. She tore down outdated fluorescent lights that flickered constantly. Recessed lights, in concert with a half dozen floor and table lamps, warmed the room. Anna painted the drab walls a soft cream and accented with hanging quilts and small framed pictures. Decorative wood shelves and cabinets replaced gray, steel racks. An oval braided area rug softened the concrete floor.

The large table—solid walnut branded with her grandfather's initials on the center drawer—dominated the room. As a little girl, she had eaten lunch on this table at the Mercantile. Now she created gifts, seasonal decorations and household accents on the worn surface. A colorful assortment of small paint bottles—oils, acrylics and watercolors—lined shelves on the back wall above a table spotted with brushes, canvases, frames, palettes, and matte board. To her left, dresser drawers organized crafting wire, tassels, fabric pens, markers, glue and such. Shelves brimming with candles, silk flowers, baskets and swags reached high above. Her grandmother's antique sewing machine and chair graced the opposite wall. They remained her most treasured keepsakes. The chair—no doubt hard and uncomfortable when her grandmother sat to make Anna's yearly Easter dress—left her sore after even a few minutes, but Anna refused to replace it. Embroidery threads, tapestry needles, fabric and lace were kept neatly by.

Soon after marrying David, Anna met the aging husband and wife who operated a floral shop for three decades in this spot. Anna secured the property before it went on the market to avoid a bidding war. The location and space offered an ideal combination. Clustered with specialty shops—including an eclectic bookstore, upscale jeweler and trendy boutique—Anna's shop drew foot traffic from downtown business people, suburban women and countless tourists. While the work area provided ample room for Anna's creativity to flourish, retail space remained purposely limited. It created a more inviting atmosphere in which to display her handiwork. And less space meant lower costs and greater sales per square foot.

Anna arrived at eight o'clock each morning, allowing two hours of uninterrupted work before the day's first customers dropped in. Thanksgiving centerpieces and Christmas ornaments awaited her final touches. She completed most holiday items six months before the seasonal crush began. Although she turned a substantial profit—a byproduct of her own ingenuity and experience from the Mercantile—the shop filled a deeper need to share her gift with others. She remained mindful of her grandfather's axiom in welcoming both friends and strangers. She garnered special satisfaction providing tourists with a treasured memento from Burlington.

The phone rang. Anna glanced at her watch. 9:00. It was David. As usual. Right on time.

"Hi, honey. What are you doing?" he asked.

"Just working. How are you?"

A year ago, his morning call remained a thoughtful gesture. But she had grown weary of what had become meaningless. After some polite, but dry conversation, Anna returned to painting ornaments. How could David not know, after four years, that she preferred to work uninterrupted in the morning?

A disconcerting pattern emerged. The phone calls. Tossing her *Travel* section into the *throw out* pile on Sunday morning. *This is your thing.*

The comment uttered in the garden continued to upset her. Anna wanted to share everything—conversation, trips, outdoor activities. To have *their* things. Together. They carried on two separate conversations, lived two separate lives—in the same place, at the same time. But this wasn't a new development. It had always been this way with David. Uneasiness settled into her stomach.

Shortly before lunch, Anna heard the familiar interaction of a mother with her twenty-something daughter. She greeted them kindly and asked if she could help. Just browsing, thank you. They took turns admiring various gifts, holding them up for each other to appreciate. Anna listened and observed their body language, the girl glancing up at her mom for approval, the mother teaching her daughter how to choose fine gifts.

Anna slipped into a melancholy mood. Her own mother had died after a courageous bout with breast cancer. Anna had organized an informal gathering in Brandon with her father and brothers over the coming weekend to commemorate the second anniversary of her passing.

Immediately following her mother's death, Anna had become very angry. Angry that her mother had been taken from her at a young age. Angry that her parents would not grow old together, that her children would never know their grandmother. Angry that the cancer had been growing inside her mother's body for years without being detected.

Anna refocused her energies, working with organizations dedicated to developing earlier detection methods, her anger turning to resolve.

The steady tap summoned Anna from the back. Drops of rain splashed off car hoods and speckled the road. Men and women caught unprepared scurried under awnings, using newspapers and briefcases as makeshift umbrellas. Anna opened the door, the dank smell of wet asphalt riding a cool breeze. She stared blankly at the falling rain for a few minutes before calling David to confirm their plans.

David looked forward to the weekly match-up on *Monday Night Football*. Despite Anna's indifference to sports, she suggested they make it a fun night. Eat a light dinner and then share snacks during the game.

"Hi, honey. Just calling to see if I should stop at the grocery store on the way home."

"If you want to, I guess…"

"We were going to fix snacks and watch the game together, remember?" Anna asked hopefully.

"Oh yeah, I remember. But I need to work at home tonight. I don't think the game's going to be very good anyway."

"Are you sure?"

"Yeah. I really need to finish this report," David replied.
"Okay. We can do it another time. I'll see you at six."

Before David had savored his last bite of pasta salad, Anna
scooped up his plate over mumbled objections. Clanking
plates, forks, spoons and bowls thrown haphazardly into the
dishwasher signaled her desire to dive into the novel. Anna
ran upstairs, shedding her work clothes in favor of navy
drawstring sweatpants, an oversized college sweatshirt and
thick, cotton socks. She grabbed the book off her nightstand
and bounded down the stairs to the kitchen. Sprite crackled
over ice cubes. She took a sip, the fizz tickling her nose, and
searched the pantry for a handful of Hershey Kisses, yelling
a quick, "You need anything, David?" before settling into the
living room. She flung her favorite afghan from its perch
atop the sofa and unfolded it with one shake. She draped it
around her and snuggled into the corner, legs curled
underneath. She carefully fit the drink between her leg and
the arm of the couch.

The pelting rain and gusting wind became a soothing
backdrop for escape. Anna immersed herself in the novel as
easily as she had sunk into the sofa. The story wove moving
pictures of a young couple forging a love affair through the
monotony of everyday life. Their struggles mirrored the
experiences of readers. The book's author, Morgan Jackson,
captured the magic of the couple's connection amidst the
mundane.

Anna dissolved into page after page, reaching blindly for
her glass, taking sips and slowly lowering it. She had
become the main character. The author was describing her,
painting vivid pictures of her dreams and the intimate
relationship she wanted. But it was far different than the life

she experienced with David. The familiar churning in her stomach returned, uneasiness mixed with longing. Seeds of doubt continued to grow. Anna reached for a drink, but heard the clinking of melted cubes circling the bottom of the glass. David called from the den.

"You ready for bed, honey?"

"Uh huh," came her muted response.

She grudgingly rose from the couch, the afghan slipping off and stopping at her waist before sliding down her legs. Anna staggered toward the kitchen, her eyes refusing to let go of the pages. She placed the glass in the sink and fumbled for the light switch, continuing her trancelike walk up to the bedroom. She slowly lowered the book to the vanity, clunking her toothbrush down and squeezing the tube with one hand. She completed her nighttime routine blindly before climbing into bed.

"Hard to put down, huh?" David asked.

Anna glanced up, placing the novel on the nightstand. David snatched the book and flipped it open.

"It will be difficult to understand the story if you don't start from the…"

"I just want to see what you're reading."

Anna studied David's expression. A furrowed brow. Skeptical, dismissive.

"Anna, this isn't real," he scoffed, tossing the book on the bed. "Marriage isn't like this…"

David's words became background noise in Anna's mind, already reeling from the disparity made clear tonight. She was not in the mood to challenge him. Nor did she think it would help.

21

Chapter 3

A FINE spray blurred the windshield, treads splattering leftover puddles spotting the country road. David worked the wipers sporadically, maneuvering through the light Saturday morning traffic on Route 7 from Burlington to Brandon. Blue skies broke in the distance. The forecast called for a crisp, sunny autumn weekend. The rhythmic beat of a top forty station filled the car. Anna peered out the window in silence.

"Anna, I know this weekend is going to be tough for you. Do you want to talk about it?"

"I was thinking how much I miss being able to pick up the phone to call her. Just to share a conversation. To hear her voice and ask her questions. I wonder how my dad gets along without her."

"He seems to be doing okay. He keeps himself busy with the store."

Her countenance turned serene. "Yeah, but they were so close, so much in love. It was really different, you know. I can remember the way they looked at each other, how they were always together."

"Aren't you romanticizing their relationship a little now that she's gone, Anna? They were just like any other married couple. I saw them fight and..."

"You don't get it, David." The words—and her glare—cut. David remained oblivious to the meaning and implications of her words beyond the discussion at hand.

"Honey, I didn't mean to..."

"Just drop it, okay? I have a lot on my mind." Disparaging her parents' relationship was insensitive at best. Doing it on the way to her mother's memorial, unforgivable. David adjusted the radio to drown the silence.

A little boy toddled round about with legs stiff, occasionally thumping flat on his rump before getting back up again. He squealed loudly, hands stretching to latch onto the flapping shirts of scurrying cousins he would never catch. They were unaware of him, of course, consumed with their own game of tag. Before the car rolled to a stop in front of the Mercantile, the children abandoned their games and sprinted jubilantly. "Auntie Anna!" they screamed. The beautiful chaos of children—a pleasant respite from a tense morning. Anna soaked up hugs from nieces and nephews while her brothers welcomed David. Anna dropped her purse on the ground and began the chase. She lost herself in their simple innocence and laughter. Running, giggling, tagging, hugging, teasing.

She spotted her father on the front porch. They exchanged a smile and the special look a father can only share with his daughter. Anna remained her father's strongest link to his wife, and could comfort her father more than anyone. She stooped to admire her nieces' new dresses, promising to braid their hair later, and showered squirming boys with

23

smooches on chubby cheeks. She picked up her purse and moved with care toward her father. They embraced for a long time before greeting the rest of the family. The brothers determined to keep the atmosphere light, though a respectful solemnity undergirded the cheery gathering of family. The familiar banter between siblings was comforting. Growing up the only girl with two older brothers, Anna learned to hold her own. Her sisters-in-law enjoyed her spirited sparring, laughing and playfully jeering their husbands.

Anna broke away to entreat her father for a leisurely walk. The big wooden doors slammed behind them. The refreshing October air washed over their faces, and they shielded their eyes from the mid-day sun. Vibrant red and orange and gold interspersed with evergreens, majestically filling the landscape against the high blue sky. Leaves teetered from their lofty perches, see-sawing to the ground. The spectacular vista inspired expressions of awe, but words proved inadequate.

Although a tad grayer with a slight hitch to his walk, her father remained strong and active. His hands still engulfed hers.

"So how is my Annabell these days?" he asked, squeezing her hand.

"I'm good, Dad." Anna smiled. She gazed up at him with admiration and sympathy. "Can I ask you a question?"

"Sure, honey. Anything."

"How badly do you miss Mom?"

Her father stared straightforward and blinked several times. A long moment passed. "Have you ever lost your best friend?"

Anna felt a lump in her throat as she clutched his forearm and buried her head into his arm, listening to him speak.

"Do you know why I have trouble sleeping? For thirty years, I drifted to sleep holding your mom, talking about you kids, the store, our dreams. That bedroom grows colder every night."

They strolled the path behind the Mercantile, stopping on the narrow footbridge. A cornucopia of fallen leaves splotched the clear waters of the brook below. Occasionally, a rock would snag a stray leaf. The cold water rushed past until the leaf dislodged and continued its journey downstream.

"You know how people say they would trade places with a loved one who died? It sounds so romantic. But I wouldn't wish this loneliness on your mother for anything." He paused and stared at the gurgling creek, patting her hand reassuringly.

"When your mom was alive, every minute apart was empty."

She knew they had loved each other, but never appreciated the depth of their relationship. Memories of knowing glances and pats and smiles completed the picture her father described.

"Dad, did you always know Mom was the one for you?"

"When I met your mom, my life changed. I changed. Forever. I never wanted anything or anyone else. Anyone else would have been settling."

"Did you go through tough times? You know, where you didn't feel the spark?"

"Sure we did. Especially after you kids were born. Takes a lot out of you. And you know how demanding it is to run a store. The romantic feelings weren't always there. We were just plain beat! But we never stopped being best friends. There were times when we felt distant, but we knew circumstances were to blame. We always found a way to connect and reassure each other. Your mom would come beside me and gently place her hand on my forearm. That was all I needed. And I would look in her eyes. She said there was a special sparkle in my eyes for her. I know it's still there. I can feel it."

Prompted by David's comments in the car, Anna fired off another question. "Did you and Mom fight?"

Her father chuckled. "Of course. We got angry at each other. Most of the time, your mom was right about things, but not always," he said smiling. "We fought—not to hurt each other—but to work things out. I'd rather fight than be indifferent any day." He stopped and faced her. "Why do you ask, Anna? Are you and David fighting?"

"No. No. We're fine. Really."

Anna shifted conversation to the changing landscape. But his words troubled her. He spoke with simple wisdom.

The chasm between what Anna wanted and what she had widened.

Anna's father stood atop a grassy knoll broken by uneven rows of white and weathered gray headstones. Soft blue skies parted beyond him, the peaceful songs of birds riding a gentle breeze. His message was brief.

"We don't mourn your mom. She is in a better place, happy and at peace. We mourn our loss. We are the ones left hollow, the ones who lost a mom, a grandmother, a best friend.

"A couple of you asked me if I felt cheated because she died so young. I had thirty-eight years with your mom. She was the only woman I ever loved. My only wish is that you could have known her that long. Because that's how long it would take to appreciate all her wonder and beauty." He exhaled and offered a reassuring smile.

"During her last year, she felt her body slipping away. She never complained about the pain, never feared death. But every night, she rested in my arms and cried herself to sleep. She said she was going to miss each of you. You were her life." Her father looked away for a moment.

"And she was mine. I'm glad you could come. This would make your mom happy."

Anna was sure she saw the sparkle.

Chapter 4

THE FRIGID air that greeted Anna's cheeks on a November morning served as a harbinger of coming snowstorms and a hectic season. The Vermont countryside—along with thousands of eager children—anxiously awaited its first wintry covering. The approaching holidays filled Anna with anticipation and dread. She treasured the season's simple pleasures. The comfort of family, decorating a freshly cut tree, the intoxicating scent of pine needles, ornaments reflecting tiny white lights, the sound of giggling and traditional Christmas songs, leaving cookies and milk for Santa. But the weeks leading up to Saint Nick's arrival were pure mayhem.

Anna clutched her morning cup of hot cocoa, hoping to dispel the chill that had crept into her shop. She shuffled toward the worktable, arms pinched to her sides, hands enveloping the mug. Her mouth hovered above the rising steam, drawing its warmth inside. She stared blankly at the ribbons and dried flowers sprawled across the table. She could not concentrate.

It was not the cold.

Winter prompted introspection. This year, however, the questions had changed. No longer was she asking how she could improve and help others. She was weighing the balance of her life with David, determining why her marriage wasn't satisfying and the root of her discontent. Had these doubts and feelings always lurked below the surface? Why wasn't she happy? She had a loving husband. A new house and a thriving business. Supportive friends and a strong family. Yet she felt empty.

Her father's words—not to mention the novels—created a striking contrast between her expectations and reality, shaking her from complacency. She had suppressed her growing dissatisfaction, dismissing warning signs as the normal cycles of any marriage.

I never lost that sparkle in my eye for your mother. Not even now.

Did David even believe in that kind of connection? Had they *ever* shared it?

I'd rather fight than be indifferent.

Indifference. It had seeped into her soul.

Not only had the questions changed, so had the implications of the answers. She was torn by her desire to be a loving wife and the inescapable conclusion that she and David had never experienced the intimacy she longed for.

Nor did she think they ever could.

Alarmed by the insight, Anna rushed to her purse, the mug clunking to the table. Her hands trembled.

The afternoon sun flickered through the windows of the quaint cabin, spreading an amber glow that welcomed Kelli and Justin. The cabin exuded the warm ambience of a winter retreat, the scent of cedar logs and remnants of past fires drawing them in further.

A rustic farm table with place settings for two and an antique oil-burning lantern flanked the small kitchen. The pine plank floors creaked as they walked into the living room. A country sofa faced a large stone fireplace begging for logs.

Justin took Kelli by the hand and led her around the corner, revealing a nook with a four-poster canopy bed. Roses and baby's breath lay strewn across the spread. She would enjoy arranging the bouquet in the crystal vase perched atop the nightstand.

Kelli could only smile. He told her they were on their way to spend the holidays with his parents. Instead, he had planned Christmas in a secluded cabin.

"You like?" he whispered, squeezing her hand.

"I love it, Justin," she said, taking in the experience. "You are so wonderful."

"Hey, get up on the bed. I want to show you something."

"Yeah, I bet you do," Kelli responded mischievously.

"No, not that. Well, at least not yet. Look. We can see the fire and hear the logs crackling from here!"

Before she had an opportunity to ask him how he had arranged the surprise, he playfully pounced, hovering above her.

"Hey, do you know what I thought we could do?" Justin asked.

"What?" she responded with a giggle. Kelli looked up at Justin, his eyes lit up. She loved this. It was her favorite part of a trip with him.

"We'll go to the grocery store after we unpack and get pasta, salad and wine. We can cook together and have a candlelight dinner. Then we can catch a movie or go see the Christmas lights downtown—oh, did I mention you can see the fire from the bed—okay, scrap the movie! Then tomorrow morning, we're going to sleep in and you will awake to a warm fire. And I may even cook breakfast if you are nice to me tonight. Then we'll bundle up good, because you know where we are going?"

Justin didn't even wait for Kelli to answer. He was talking faster and faster, his enthusiasm drawing her in.

"There's a Christmas tree farm a few miles down the road. And you can't celebrate Christmas without a fresh tree. So we'll go to the farm, trod out and look at a thousand trees or so until you find the perfect one." That quip prompted a smirk and an elbow.

"Then I'll cut it down and drag it through the snow to the truck. We'll bring it back and let it dry out. Tomorrow afternoon, we can browse antique shops and then take a nap together by the fire. At night, we can decorate the tree. I brought ornaments and lights and our angel. Plus I thought we'd string popcorn—make it a traditional, old-fashioned Christmas.

"Did I mention that the bed has a view of the fireplace?" Justin asked, still hovering, eyes expectant.

"Several times, yes," she replied dryly. Kelli couldn't help but look up with adoration.

"Okay, so then on Christmas Eve," he continued, "we can bake Christmas cookies. Reindeer and bells and trees with sprinkles. And chocolate chip, too. Santa won't visit without cookies, you know. Then we can make stockings for each other so we'll remember this Christmas forever."

Kelli wrapped her arms around Justin's neck and gazed into his eyes, her lips touching his slightly. "I'm not going to need a stocking to remember this, you big, lovable man, you."

After a slow, deep kiss, Kelli asked coyly, "Hey, could we enjoy that view of the fireplace you so casually mentioned before?"

It was a Christmas Anna had once imagined. But one she would never experience with David.

Anna's shop overflowed with holiday crafts, ornaments and keepsakes. She had earned a reputation for creating quality, hand-made gifts. Because she sold only original pieces, neighbors shopped with confidence, assured that a prized purchase would not be found gracing the walls of a friend's home. The spirit of the Mercantile lived on through her gifts and the special manner with which Anna treated her customers.

Customer service isn't important. People are. Her grandfather's axiom guided her.

The sign on the door welcomed passersby. A portly man in his late thirties strode by, then stopped and peered through the window. He doubled back, pushing open the door decorated with a wreath and fresh garland. Although women comprised her regular staple of customers, men knew the shop was a safe place to purchase presents for their loved ones.

Anna sized him up as he began a routine common to most men, a routine she found enchanting. He wandered the store, studying various items before setting them down, pretending to know exactly what he was looking for. Slowly but surely, signs of frustration broke through the charade, his face flush.

He unbuttoned his overcoat and loosened the scarf, the sweat on his brow caused more by anxiety than warmth.

This was Anna's cue to move in. She had perfected her ritual. With a little coaxing, she could sell a man filled with self-doubt anything she desired—from the most expensive keepsake to the most imaginative creation—and he would walk away confident he had the perfect gift for his wife in hand. But she never took advantage of the men. With a sweetness that belied the devilish feelings inside, Anna asked, "Do you need some help?"

"Sure," he allowed, a little embarrassed.

"Are you shopping for your wife?"

"Yes. Something special for Christmas."

"What does she like?"

Like most men, he was clueless, offering the usual, "Well, you know, something really pretty or nice."

Fortunately, Anna knew many of the men's wives—and their tastes in decorating. If not, she knew the right questions to ask. Confidently walking to a shelf, Anna picked up an appropriate gift, looked the man in the eyes and said in a hushed tone, "I think she might like this." He would shrug and nod, the sale complete. Her knowing look and reassuring manner put the man at ease for another year. This scene would repeat itself often over the next month.

Anna snuck bites of turkey and swiss between the constant stream of customers that followed. Her patrons included friends and acquaintances she had not seen in months. She cherished pictures of sons and daughters, sharing stories and promising to meet soon for lunch.

◆◆◆

The darkening sky signaled the end of another long day. Anna retreated to the back of her shop. But even rekindled friendships could not assuage the discord within. She felt no urgency to go home, no desire to see her husband. Her fingers searched the pages.

A piece of paper folded over. Slid under the pillow, to be discovered when Kelli made the bed. Justin had been working late every night. She picked up the paper, a question scribbled across the top.

"Do you know how much I want to be with you?"

A picture drawn in pencil below. A four-legged animal. All of Justin's drawings looked the same, some variation of a horse or cow. Horses were taller, the cows plumper. This creature was shorter. She looked closely, noting the faint outlines of erased markings. An artist he was not.

Below the animal, the answer written in bold letters.

"BAAAAAADDLLYY."

Kelli laughed out loud. It must be a sheep, she thought. She sniffled and wiped away a small tear. Without words, he knew exactly what she needed. The depth of his love—and the fact that he knew her better than anyone ever had—enabled Kelli to rest content and give herself to him completely.

It was simple. It was small. It was meaningful.

She carried the dumb picture with her the rest of the day.

◆◆◆

The novels illuminated Anna's hopes and dreams, revealing a life she longed to experience. A life she once thought possible. A jingle, and loud voice shouting through the store, startled her.

"What are you doing, Anna banana?" the young woman asked, her scarf and hat flying off in one motion, barely finding its way to the table. Had it not been her best friend, Anna would have hated this greeting. But this was Susan. Obnoxious and overbearing at times, but a loyal and caring friend—a rare find.

"Hey, Suz." Anna's reply lacked enthusiasm.

"What's wrong? Business slow today?"

"The opposite. I didn't have time to stop for a lunch break. Probably just tired, that's all."

Susan hesitated for a moment, then leaned across the table. "You've been reading those books again, haven't you?" she asked, the question mixed with equal parts accusation and expectation. Anna had tried to interest her in reading them. But Susan wasn't one to sit more than a few minutes without opening her mouth. She preferred to get the highlights from Anna.

Anna glanced down, hiding a slight smile, her preoccupation exposed. Still, it comforted her to know that at least *someone* knew her so well. "Maybe," she replied defiantly.

Anna looked up, her expression troubled, catching Susan off guard. "Something is happening with David. I mean, between David and me."

"Did he do something to you?" Susan asked, moving closer.

"No, it's not that at all." Anna struggled for the right words. "I'm not sure I'm in love with him."

"Anna, of course you love, David. Why would you even say that?"

"I know I love him. I mean, I care about him. I do. But I am not excited to be with him. I'm not sure I ever have been."

"Come on, Anna. David is a great guy. He's a good husband, he's..." Susan's words trailed off. Anna stood motionless, stunned by her own words. It marked the first time she had given voice to these thoughts.

I am not in love with him.

It was true.

And everything Susan said was true. David was a good man, handsome, thoughtful. He would be a good father to their children. He was, by all accounts, what most women desired in a man. Which is why it remained difficult to explain her dissatisfaction without appearing ungrateful. The familiar refrain throbbed:

Don't you realize how lucky you are to have such a good man?

"Susan, I know what you are saying. Don't you think I have thought about that a million times? There's something missing."

"Do you think your expectations are too high, Anna?"

Having tortured herself with these same questions, Anna grew irritated at having to justify her perspective. "Susan, is it too much to expect to share passion for each other? I want to have that connection with my husband."

"Have you tried?"

"Yes, I try to draw him into activities, to share experiences. But he doesn't think like that. I'm not sure he's capable of it."

Anna admitted she had serious reservations about David before they married. He lacked imagination and the ability to make her laugh, two qualities Anna treasured. But she could not bear to second-guess herself now.

"Anna, you have everything. You're living the American dream."

"But, Susan," she replied heavily, "it's not *my* dream."

Chapter 5

EVEN THE newspaper seemed stiff this morning, crinkling as Anna turned the pages. To call it a newspaper was a misnomer. As in most small towns, newsworthy events remained sparse. Human-interest stories, obituaries and community happenings attracted attention. Not to mention the police blotter. Attempted break-in. Vandalism. Emotionally disturbed person three hundred block of E. Main. Destruction of private property six hundred block of E. Main. Some street to live on. Suspicious activity. Drunk and disorderly. A busy night for the city's finest.

Anna sought comfort in her morning ritual. She raised her mug of cocoa, glancing past the cover articles about local zoning commission rulings and Rotary Club meetings. A hard gulp. Her eyes widened. A name in bold letters. Morgan Jackson.

If the cocoa had not awakened her, this notice had. Sitting up and moving closer to the paper, Anna read with disbelief the announcement from Canterbury College. The school had secured Morgan Jackson as the featured speaker at the Guest Lecture Series when classes resumed in January. This was quite a coup. Mr. Jackson made few public appearances and shunned the limelight. A former classmate had persuaded

Mr. Jackson to share his insight with the young writers in the area. An accompanying article detailed the two novels he had written, each of which Anna constantly reread.

She held the paper's edge and ripped out the notice. She stared at it blankly for a moment before tossing it aside. I shouldn't go, she thought. After the previous night's confession to Susan, Anna reevaluated her relationship with David. They were comfortable together and got along well. People remarked that she and David looked happy. All marriages go through difficult times, right? Maybe it's me. Maybe I'm focusing on the wrong things.

She considered putting the books away. They continued to trouble her, drawing wider the disparity between what she had and what she wanted. But, she wondered whether they had caused this disparity or merely revealed the emptiness.

Anxious shoppers milled about outside, hoping to get an early start on the day's shopping. Anna obliged, opening the store early rather than making her customers stand in the cold. Another hectic day ensued. But she remained distracted by the possibility of meeting Morgan Jackson in less than four weeks.

Late that afternoon, Anna decided to stop reading the novels, ignore the anxious thoughts and focus instead on improving her marriage. Christmas and a New Year loomed, a time to be hopeful.

The sky stretched in unending gray across the horizon. Billowing clouds overlapped in unbroken succession to fashion a patchwork ceiling. Strains of a pale sun filtered through, casting an ominous shroud above the Burlington landscape. Ideal for sleeping in on a lazy Saturday morning. The glowing numbers read 9:37. Anna slumped under the down comforter. David stretched and yawned. She scooted closer to him—there was no such thing as being too warm during a Vermont winter.

The room remained dark. Only the persistent whir of the fan broke the silence. No cars rattling or dogs barking or children shrieking. No phones ringing, no television or radio blaring. Just the soothing buzz from the corner. The bed sucked them into lethargy. They had no plans for the day, nothing that would compel them to leave the comfort.

Anna propped herself on elbows and gave David a kiss on the cheek. "Good morning, honey," she sighed in her still-half-asleep voice.

"Morning," David responded, managing to open one eye. "You sleep well?"

"Yeah, but I think I could sleep all day." Anna had slept peacefully for the first time in what seemed like months. She had relaxed and enjoyed their night together. Every Friday after work, Anna and David met at the video store to rent movies. They drove home, threw on sweats and ordered Chinese. While David made the short trip to pick up dinner, Anna readied the movies and drinks. They lounged and savored their favorite dishes while watching the first movie. Halfway through the second, they hit pause and scampered to the kitchen for ice cream. It was comfortable and relaxing and Anna settled into it. This isn't so bad, she had thought.

"I didn't keep you up too late, did I?" David asked naughtily.

The thought his question stirred jolted Anna from her serenity. Sex with David was disappointing and typified their relationship—predictable with no passion and little understanding of her needs. She preferred to brush it aside.

"What do you want to do today?" she asked.

"Well, I was going to change the furnace filters. Do you need to do any shopping?"

"No, but I have an idea."

"What is it?"

Anna faced David, elbow on pillow, right hand supporting her head. Her eyes brightened as she began. "I thought we could go get a fresh tree together this afternoon. There's this huge tree farm outside of Montpelier where we can chop our own. They have hot cider and cookies and reindeer we can feed. It would be a fun way to get into the Christmas spirit."

"I guess we could. But the Boy Scouts are selling them down at the corner. Wouldn't it be easier to grab one there?"

Anna cringed.

"What's wrong?" David asked.

I'd rather fight than be indifferent.

"David, I wanted to do something special—something fun and different. Does everything have to be some task we check off a list? Instead of picking up a tree, let's make it an event and enjoy the experience. Do you know what I mean?"

"I'm sorry, honey. I'll try harder. Why don't we do that?"

Try harder. It's not in him. He's doing it to please me. Well, at least he *is* trying. She ignored the thoughts and decided to enjoy the day.

"Good! It will be fun. Why don't you hop in the shower and I'll start breakfast."

Anna grabbed the rumpled heap of sweats and socks off the floor, watching David walk toward the bathroom. She cursed under her breath, frustrated at herself for asking too much of him. As Christmas neared, she resolved to be grateful.

◆ ◆ ◆

"Auntie Anna! Auntie Anna!" A gaggle of tiny hands tugged at her legs. Little outstretched arms thrust high above heads beseeched her. Anna and David stumbled through the front door, nieces and nephews and brothers and sisters-in-law and father crammed into the foyer, offering hugs and hearty Merry Christmases. A stack of presents balanced under her chin toppled to the floor, beautifully wrapped gifts in all shapes and sizes with ribbons and bows crashing around the feet of pajama-clad toddlers. David and Anna knelt, winter jackets spun from their arms and hung in the closet. The boys and girls swarmed them, squealing with delight.

"Can we open our gifts now?"

The children had risen before the sun, anxious to tear into presents. The families began a tradition of sleeping in the same house on Christmas Eve so the cousins could wake and open gifts together. Fortunately, Santa had filled their stockings with enough candy, gum and crayons to hold them at bay until Anna and David arrived.

Anna looked sympathetically at her brothers and their wives. Anna and David appeared fresh and showered, dressed neatly. The rest of the family remained in sleeping attire. The women gathered, coffee mugs in hand, hair pulled back. The men cavorted with the kids, comfortable as usual with hair mussed or covered by baseball caps. Dark circles hung under weary eyes from midnight adventures assembling bicycles and the pre-dawn awakening to little ones romping. But no complaints could be heard in the Matthews household. Only smiles and laughter and the boundless enthusiasm of children on Christmas morning. Music played softly in the background as the fire crackled. It was magic.

The children sprawled across the living room floor, awaiting the signal to begin. "Who ate the cookies and drank the milk?" Anna gasped, hands over mouth, pointing to the crumb-laden plate and empty glass by the fireplace.

"Santa Claus!" came the resounding chorus of high-pitched voices.

"And Wu-doff ate the cawwot," chimed the four-year-old in ponytails.

The adults took their seats and prepared for pandemonium. They would have time to talk and exchange gifts later. But the real Christmas—the one that captivated the hearts of children and adults alike—was poised to begin.

For a moment all voices hushed while a flurry of tiny fingers ripped wrapping paper off the first gifts. Cameras flashed. Anna surveyed the room. The adults, beaming with joy, delighted in the wonder lighting their children's faces. "Look Mommy! Look Daddy!" they shrieked before casting aside one gift for the next. Unwelcome presents like clothes were discarded quickly in favor of finding something fun. Paper and plastic and cardboard littered the carpet. Bows and ribbons—so carefully placed beforehand—so carelessly tossed into the piles. Her brothers scooped up the trash with roving hands, revealing a mini playground of toys, dolls and brightly colored clothes.

Anna's eyes lit up, reveling in the excitement of her nieces and nephews. She nestled next to David and asked softly, "Would you rather have a baby boy or girl first?"

David sat stoically taking in the scene. "I don't know, honey. I guess I haven't given it much thought." He kissed her head and rose to walk to the kitchen. "I'm going to get some coffee. Do you want some?"

Anna's heart sank. He didn't see the magic, only the mess.

Chapter 6

THE NEWSPAPER clipping lay askew on the edge of the worktable. The remnants of projects completed before Christmas remained scattered, left unkempt in the rush to begin the holidays. Anna straightened up—placing scissors in the drawer, ribbons and bows in their box, paints on the appropriate shelf—and tossed scraps of paper and material into the trash bin. She worked around the clipping, unable to throw it away. It had tempted her for weeks. She picked it up again and stared. Morgan Jackson. She placed it back down and walked to the front of the store.

Anna climbed into the showcase window and removed Christmas decorations. A sentimental chord struck. No more yuletide songs and merry wishes. Santas, wreaths, garland and all things red and green stored neatly in marked boxes for another ten months. The streets were decidedly empty, the rush—and the bounce—absent from people's strides. The promise of Christmas eased the sting of winter's first frigid blasts. Spring remained an eternity away—it did not arrive in Vermont on March twenty-first. The brutal onslaught of Mother Nature could continue into April.

Unlike most merchants, Anna did not mark down Christmas items. She refused to diminish their inherent value and create the perception they were overpriced. She knew her customers' tastes and managed inventories wisely. Word-of-mouth recommendations drove new customers through the front door and Christmas sales rose dramatically again. Lessons learned from the Mercantile.

With less shop traffic during January, Anna enjoyed the time to create, work she missed during the Thanksgiving and Christmas rush. She reflected on popular designs from the prior year and searched for insight into coming trends. She began rotating the selection of gifts and keepsakes to meet demand for Valentine's Day, breaking at noon.

Anna spread her lunch on the large table. The announcement troubled her. She crumpled it and tossed it to the floor.

The picture became clearer every day. So did the implications. This author and his novels prompted visions of a life far different. The kind of relationship she wanted. Or had she discovered that she *needed* it? Finding the answers to the questions threatened her security. She could not hide from the truth. Anna knew she could live a "good life" with David. Comfortable. Easy. No changes.

But her father's words resounded.

Anyone else would have been settling.

Anna leaned over and grabbed the clipping off the floor. Before she had eaten half her sandwich, she unfolded the paper, making sure the phone number remained legible.

She dialed the number. Her hand trembled. One ring. She slammed the phone down. Anna stepped back and took a deep breath.

Through glassy eyes, she stared at the name on the page, lamenting that she was asking David to be someone he could not be. But she would regret missing this opportunity to meet

Morgan Jackson. The books were affecting her. She needed to know why.

She picked up the phone again, this time more steadily. Come on. Answer. Please let there be tickets left.

A pleasant woman answered. "Just a minute, please, let me check." Anna thought about the day she and David cut the Christmas tree. He had agreed to go, but it wasn't his first instinct. To David, one day led to the next. He didn't understand the need to transform ordinary tasks into experiences. They were two separate people. Moving in opposite directions. With disparate aspirations. Her thoughts were interrupted by the woman reporting gladly that tickets remained.

Anna breathed a sigh of relief. But securing the ticket only intensified the struggle.

Onions sautéing in olive oil crackled above the soft melody streaming from the living room. Anna continued humming, mincing fresh garlic and dropping tiny pieces into the pan. Spices, fresh vegetables and sharp knives covered a worn cutting board. A silver ladle, wooden spoon and myriad utensils spotted the granite counter. Anna stirred until the onions turned translucent and the garlic golden brown. A burst of sweetness sprang from tomatoes plunging into the mix. Anna sipped her Chianti and closed her eyes. She enjoyed surprising David with a special meal. The stress lifted. Anna tossed in green peppers and mushrooms and accented with spices, leaving the sauce to simmer for a couple of hours until he arrived.

Anna raced upstairs, unwilling to waste a second of her time alone. She ran a bubble bath and hunted for matches. Spying the novel on her nightstand, she paused to read.

Justin dumped the contents of the brown bag on his desk, sandwich sliding out, chips poking through the baggie and apple thudding. His eyes remained glued to the computer screen, once again working through lunch. Reaching blindly for the sandwich, Justin found a piece of paper instead. He smiled and turned his undivided attention to the stick figure drawings and poem.

An arrow for a bow.
A puppy for a child.
Peanut butter for jelly.
You for me.
Nothing is complete by itself.
I am thankful you are the one for me.
Kelli.

Anna wished she could say the same about David. She craved the passion. She closed the book and sighed, wondering whether she had done the right thing today.

Anna immersed herself in the steaming tub, a shiver running down her spine at first touch before melting into the heat. The airy bubbles and undulating water left her feeling weightless. Cranberry and holly candles bordered the tub and vanity, flickering across the room. Anna gently caressed her arms and neck in the soothing warmth, reclining her head and drifting off.

She awoke to the pungent aroma of garlic and basil. She soaked for a few minutes longer before climbing from the tub and slipping on a comfortable pair of jeans and red cotton sweater.

Waltzing into the kitchen, Anna surveyed her work. She stirred the simmering sauce with a wooden spoon, noting the texture and color. Placing a hand under the spoon, she slowly drew it to her mouth. She lightly smacked and licked her lips. A pinch of salt and pepper followed. David would be home any minute. She placed dirty utensils in the sink and returned spices to cupboards while retrieving pots and strainers for the noodles. The box of pasta toppled over. The long, thin strands slid unevenly onto the counter.

The phone rang. Anna answered. The Fraternal Order of Police was conducting its annual fundraiser. Yes, of course, I will help. Water bubbled and gurgled, sloshing over the top of the large pot onto the red burner with spurting hisses. As she finished her conversation, steam gushed in torrents toward the ceiling. The air became humid, salty. Condensation formed on the vent. Anna slid across the hardwood floor, moving the pot and clicking on the fan.

"Hi, honey!" David yelled, walking through the door.

"Hey," Anna managed. "How was your day?"

"Good." David poked his head around the corner. "Smells delicious."

"Why don't you go up and change?"

"Okay. Be right back down."

"Would you like wine or milk?"

"Wine," she heard as David scampered upstairs.

She stooped to check the garlic bread before dipping the cooked pasta in the sauce for a final taste. Just right. She set the table and reached in the cupboard for a wine glass. As David came downstairs, Anna poured his drink and refreshed her own.

"You know those novels I've been reading?" she began, handing David his Chianti.

"Uh huh," came the expected reply.

"Well, the author, Morgan Jackson, is speaking at Canterbury College next week." She allowed the statement to sink in, observing his body language to gauge his response. None. "I purchased a ticket today for next Tuesday night at seven."

"That's good, honey. You should enjoy that." David leaned in toward her on the way to the refrigerator. "Maybe you can find out what his *magic* is," he said derisively.

She never asked David to read the books, but occasionally read him excerpts, hoping to spark his curiosity and offer more intimate ideas than flowers, dinner and a movie. But he dismissed the books as unrealistic tales. Just as he had dismissed the depth of her parents' relationship.

David launched into a stale account of his day at work. He droned on about tax law and issues so tedious even scholars would struggle to comprehend. Could you try saying that in English, she thought. But she listened attentively and asked questions because his work was important to him. To David, conversation consisted of regurgitating facts and trivial details. Anna watched his mouth move, but his words became background noise. He didn't know what interested her. He never dreamed with her.

Discussion turned to dinner. David finished chopping the vegetables and mixed them into two salad bowls. Here was a positive. They liked the same food, worked well together at home and were comfortable with their routines. Anna poured sauce over tangled noodles alongside steaming bread. From the outside, the picture of them cooking together recalled a Norman Rockwell painting.

But reality spoiled the glimpse of hope. They stood side-by-side, but remained worlds apart. They were two people who had simply grown accustomed to living together.

Anna longed for more than comfort. She needed the connection.

◆◆◆

Anna brushed the dusting of snow from her windows with bare hands. She had forgotten her mittens this morning, her mind elsewhere. Climbing into the car, she blasted the heat and placed her red hands against the vents. The warm air stung at first, then soothed. She had closed the shop early, hoping to beat the afternoon traffic and imminent snowstorm. The seventy-minute drive to Middlebury could take twice as long if the storm hit at rush hour. Mr. Jackson's lecture was scheduled to begin at seven o'clock. Anna needed to go home, grab a bite to eat and change clothes before traveling south.

Her hands warmed to an even temperature. She moved them from the heater to the radio, scanning the stations impatiently for an updated weather forecast. *Clouds clearing out by early morning tomorrow, but not until...* Anna flipped stations, needing tonight's forecast. All she heard most other days were weather forecasts repeated ad nauseam. But today, she continued to catch the end of each report up and down the dial. She switched to AM. *Your weather coming up after this break.*

The day dragged at the shop. About the only thing Anna accomplished was staring at her watch every ten minutes. She started projects, but could not concentrate long enough to complete them. After lunch, she switched to tasks requiring little thought—filing, organizing, cleaning.

Snow is on the way. Meteorologist Dan Duvall has more from the Skywatch 2 Weather Center. That's right, Bob, we have a fast-moving system speeding toward the Champlain Valley. Some parts of Burlington picked up a dusting today from the leading edges of the storm. Areas west are reporting that heavy snow is falling and we expect it to hit Burlington within the hour. The real problem will be tonight during rush hour and into early evening. We could see snow falling at the rate of an inch or more per hour before tapering off later tonight. Total accumulations of four to six inches are expected. Road crews are poised to begin spreading salt and plowing, which will continue overnight. Tomorrow morning's drive to work should be uneventful. Please be careful out there. Bob, back to you.

Large flakes swooped against her windshield, melting on contact. Anna headed north to Colchester on Route 89. The flakes grew more tightly formed, filling the sky, falling with greater intensity. Grayish white clouds swarmed above. Gusts blew snow sideways across the car. By the time Anna reached her subdivision, a powdery blanket covered the streets.

Anna clicked the garage remote repeatedly from half a block away, anxious to get inside to prepare for the night's event. She fixed herself a sandwich and scurried upstairs to freshen up and change clothes, catching glimpses of the strengthening storm. Trees, shrubs and mailboxes donned a fresh cover.

David arrived home unexpectedly about a half hour later. Anna heard him running up the stairs.

"Hi, honey. The roads are getting really slick now."

"How was your day?" Anna was in her own world.

She continued her feverish pace, sneaking bites of her sandwich while changing clothes, freshening makeup, slipping on shoes and trying on earrings.

"You aren't still planning to go tonight, are you?" David asked, his tone gauged to dissuade her.

"Uh huh," she nodded nonchalantly.

"Honey, it will be dangerous until the plows have a chance to clear the roads. Do you know how hard it's supposed to…"

Anna fastened her earrings and sprayed her hair, hearing his voice but not his words.

"Anna, you can't go out on a night like…"

"I'll be fine. Don't worry," Anna replied, walking past David for a final glance in the mirror.

"Well, then I'll drive you down there. I can take something to do while you…"

Anna gave David a kiss on the cheek and hurried down the stairs. "I have to go. I'll see you later, okay?"

"Sure you don't want a ride?" she heard as the door slammed behind her.

Thirty seconds later, the door burst open. She grabbed her book off the kitchen counter and ran back to the car.

Anna wound through the subdivision, stopping hard to test the brakes and get a feel for the road. She glanced at the clock. 5:15. She turned right just past the gate. Although an unwelcome obstacle, Anna considered the falling snow a challenge—growing up traversing Vermont's wintry lanes gave her confidence.

Making it through the first two lights, she accelerated. One more light and she could catch the ramp to Highway 89, the major interstate running through Burlington. Once south of the city, she would pick up Route 7 for the remainder of the trip. The light turned yellow. Anna was still sixty feet away. Moving too fast to stop safely, she held the steering wheel rigid and winced as her Volvo screamed through the intersection. Her relief was dispelled by the patch of red brake lights inching forward on 89. She eased onto the ramp. The clump of lights became a sea of red in one direction and white approaching. She groaned and turned on the radio for updated traffic and weather reports. 5:35.

In the frustrating monotony of crawling south, Anna's thoughts turned to tonight's event. What did she expect from a stranger? Magical answers to the disturbing questions? She knew it wouldn't be that simple. But intuition insisted she be there.

6:15. She was going to be late. Cars and trucks peeled off exit ramps. Anna spotted the signs for Route 7 South. The road's twists and turns made for peaceful autumn afternoon romps, but perilous January nights. 6:30. Anna flipped her windshield wipers to high. She could no longer discern individual flakes in the beams of oncoming cars. It appeared as if God had turned the heavens upside down and dumped the winter's allocation of snow in one giant heave.

Anna gripped the wheel. Tension stung her shoulders. The defroster's cold air cleared the encroaching condensation, but sent a chill down her neck. Trucks splashing buckets of dirty slush across the windshield blinded her. She shifted her body and hunted for a clear view. 6:48. Wiper fluid intended to melt ice merely left blue streaks trailing. She searched her mirrors, stealing glances at the clock. 6:55. Anna panicked.

A salt truck thundered past, its booming plow scraping the pavement, grooming a narrow path. Salt crunched under her tires and pinged against the undercarriage. Anna accelerated and relaxed her shoulders. Middlebury lie beyond the approaching town. 7:12. The road snaked through a short stretch without lights. Anna glanced at the clock, each passing minute a lost opportunity to hear Morgan Jackson speak. 7:24. Traffic thinned and Anna cautiously increased her speed.

Coming out of a bend, red brake lights filled her eyes. The car ahead must have been crawling at fifteen miles per hour, Anna thirty-five. Anna closed the gap too quickly and jerked the wheel to the right. The car slid sideways, like a rubber tube on an icy hill. She clenched the steering wheel, her face cringing and body bracing for impact. There was none. The car stopped, spun sideways straddling two lanes. Anna gathered herself and crept forward, resuming her trip. 7:48. She remained shaken by the possibility of missing Morgan Jackson.

Anna cursed each stop light in Middlebury. At 8:14, she zipped into the first empty parking spot at the college, sliding to a crooked stop, hitting the lights and yanking keys from the ignition in one motion. She raced through the snow-covered lot, hands buried in her coat, purse flopping against her side and back. The wind ripped the heat from her body and made her eyes water. The calm of the campus under falling snow stood in stark contrast to the anxiety gripping Anna. She implored the heavens again for help.

Anna reached the library gasping and heaved open the large doors. The wind howled through the opening. She marched through the familiar atrium, eyes fixed. A quick glimpse at her watch. 8:24. Ugghh. Anna pressed on, jogging up a winding stairway. She felt thoroughly disheveled— inside and out. A signpost down the corridor pointed to the room where Mr. Jackson had been scheduled to speak. Could he still be there? College students huddled outside the room. Good. She ran down the hallway, long coat trailing.

Anna rushed into the room, eyes wide and searching. People milled about, clumped in groups of two and three, leaning on chairs, absorbed in light-hearted conversation. Most appeared to be college girls. She spotted a long line.

"Excuse me," she asked a young woman. "Is this the line to meet Morgan Jackson?"

"Yes, it is."

She took her place in line. Just like the traffic tonight. Anna strained to catch a glimpse of Mr. Jackson, to no avail.

She feared that she missed something important tonight, but was relieved to have an opportunity to meet him. She tapped her feet, surveying the room. Hand-carved walnut molding bordered cream plaster ceilings etched in an elaborate motif. Large oil portraits of past college presidents and benefactors graced hunter green walls. A pair of exquisite chandeliers hung proudly above the hardwood floors, light glistening off wood-paned windows. Coats lay folded across the backs of stodgy wooden chairs. The seats were divided into two sections, each of which filled approximately eight rows with ten chairs each.

Anna returned her attention to the line. She bit her lip in nervous anticipation, counting the fans ahead of her. Ten people. Nine women, one man. The steady buzz of conversation hung in the air. Anna sighed, contemplating the obstacles she had overcome to make it here. First battling the internal struggle and then the snowstorm. Stuck in the back of a line, alone amongst strangers. Just to exchange greetings and converse awkwardly with an unknown author while he signs the book, then drive home over treacherous roads late on a work night.

Her expectation grew as the line thinned. The man sitting a few feet away had written stories in which she had become the main character. The sweat on her palms loosened her grip on the book. Anna lifted on tiptoes, still unable to see the author. An eternity passed before the line withered to a handful of students. Anna leaned on one leg and peered around the women in front of her. She could make out the wavy brown hair of a man scribbling his name into a novel. She stared at him.

He glanced up.

Their eyes met.

"Evan?"

Chapter 7

"ANNA."

The book plunged to the floor with a thud. She knelt, legs trembling and arms limp, eyes unable to focus. Anna tried to steady herself as she rose. She crossed her arms to conceal quivering hands, clutching the book hard to her chest. He attempted to mask his preoccupation, but could not will his eyes from her. She grew self-conscious under his gaze, her eyes darting and mouth faltering. An uncomfortable fever pulsed in waves from her face to her stomach. Rational thoughts foundered, unable to mollify the force of emotion.

Time stood still as the collective mosaic of friendship, passion and love—forged through years of shared experiences—fused into a single moment. Disjointed memories collided with haunting sentiments, even smells and sounds, leaving her disoriented. Anna shuffled forward. Three people stood between them. She could see him fully— his eyes, his mouth, his hands. His voice held her captive to the past.

They had not spoken in eight years. She felt vulnerable. He could crush her with indifference or disapproval. Her eyes danced about as she studied him, her legs shifting. Only two people ahead. Her heart raced into her throat, the thumping audible. Her mouth was parched.

One woman stood between them. Anna breathed deeply and cleared her throat, brushing a strand of hair from her face. The woman received her signed book and moved to the right with a thank you. Anna stepped forward tentatively, her eyes swollen with affection, revealing a tenderness she had not felt in years.

"Why haven't you written to me, Evan?"

"I have been, Anna," he replied gently. "I have been."

Anna staggered away, undone. She made her way to the hallway, collapsing against a wall, slumping to the floor. Students, signs, doorways blurred. Tears raced down her cheeks in competing streams, the stinging salt reassuring Anna that her heart remained capable of loving deeply. She refused to wipe the tears.

A confusing maze of questions and images cluttered her mind. She recalled the first time she saw him. The way he smiled at her. Talking and laughing in the campus courtyard. The thoughtful notes, his stories, their dreams. Saying goodbye, the bitter tears, her heart broken.

A petite woman with gray hair and glasses drew near and placed her book before him. "What a pleasure it is to meet you, Mr. Jackson." Evan looked down sheepishly to pen his signature. His hand trembled. The sight of Anna had melted him. He forced his way through the obligatory niceties, but his eyes were searching for her.

Her voice stirred memories of scenes he had relived countless times. Strolling with her arm wrapped in his, the thrill of her laugh, the sweet way she cuddled and kissed his chin, long drives filled with conversation. She was so close.

Evan glanced repeatedly toward the hallway, unnerved by uncertainty. Would she be there when he finished? The end of the line. A college student approached. Evan graciously accepted her portfolio and promised to read her work. Rising to his feet, Evan marched forward searching for Anna. The event coordinator dashed behind him. "Mr. Jackson! Mr. Jackson!" Evan wheeled around to face the young man. "Are you okay, Mr. Jackson?"

"Oh, of course. Thank you," he muttered, shaking the man's hand and resuming his pursuit.

The strength of emotion was foreign, simultaneously comforting and disturbing. She had come expecting clarity. She found dark shadows. Memories collided. A hopeful voice interrupted.

"Anna."

She looked up at the author, the man she had fallen in love with as a young woman. She was unable to speak.

"How are you, Anna?" Evan asked.

"I'm fine, Evan," she replied softly, her eyes wide and searching, absorbing every detail. The lines on his face were more defined, but his eyes still penetrated. He offered his hand as she slowly rose to her feet, but Anna did not take it. They stood awkwardly facing each other, grappling with the desire to embrace, restrained by circumstance.

She wanted to imagine that she was not married, that the past eight years had not happened and that they were together, looking forward to the future. But she couldn't. There were too many questions. She *was* married.

Evan stood, humbled to be near her. His hands fidgeted, fighting the natural urge to caress her skin and feel the softness of her hair, to explore the wonder of her eyes and her lips tender and warm. She fought every instinct to surrender to the shelter of his arms, his embrace thawing her indifference.

"Anna, I've thought about..." he began. His voice, intimate and yet far away, drew her.

"No, Evan, I can't talk. Not now. I'm married." Her heart sank, aware that her statement hurt him, regretting that she had married David.

"I know," Evan replied solemnly. The words, the tone pierced her. Anna imagined the sting of discovering Evan was sharing his life with another.

But, oh, the way he said it. No self-pity or pain in his voice. He spoke with empathy, knowing that saying it hurt *her* more than him. He hadn't changed. And with those two words, he told her he wasn't married. She saw it in his deep blue eyes, the far off look, the longing.

"I have to go, Evan. I have to go."

He scribbled a note and placed it in her hand, asking her to call. Without answering, Anna turned from him.

Chapter 8

ANNA FUMBLED with clanking keys, steadying her hand long enough to unlock the door. She slumped into the seat and sobbed. Reluctantly, she started the engine, glanced over her shoulder through bleary eyes and backed out of the parking space. The snow had stopped. So had her world. She left the campus where she had met Evan ten years ago.

He wandered past her on a sunny morning in March, wearing jeans, hiking boots and an old sweatshirt, which, judging by the numerous holes and worn letters, had been a staple of his wardrobe for some time. At first glance, he appeared similar to all the young men at the college, fairly attractive she thought, but really no different from the others. After searching the bookstore—she couldn't recall what he purchased—he approached the checkout counter. He greeted her with gentle voice and bashful smile, gazing for a moment into her eyes, revealing something genuine in his own. Still, Anna didn't give him another thought until his visits became frequent, and his eyes lingered.

He would meander through the door and catch her glance, then stride to the middle of the store where textbooks rested on beige metal shelves rising slightly below his chin. His distraction was clear—Anna caught him peeking at her every so often. At first, he dropped his eyes in seeming embarrassment. Soon he was holding her gaze. And he never failed to pick up a pack of gum or a candy bar—so he could talk to her, she thought. It started innocently, mostly small talk and smiles. He finally introduced himself. Evan. Increasingly she felt comforted by his warmth, enthralled by his ability to make her laugh. The fact that he never asked her out intrigued Anna. Before long, Anna's roommates noticed her primping in the morning, humming and oddly anxious to leave for work, spiraling curls replacing the convenient ponytail.

She eagerly anticipated his daily visits, days made complete by their moments together. She enjoyed the simple conversation, absent of pressure. He would lean against the counter, speaking in hushed tones and whispers, the silence shattered by bursts of laughter. When shoppers entered, Evan disappeared amongst merchandise, peeking out to divert her attention. It became a playful game, Evan goading her to giggle in front of customers and Anna doing her best to suppress her laugh—and her obvious fondness for this boy.

After weeks of casual flirting, Evan began lingering until her shift ended so he could walk Anna to her car. Their relationship blossomed beyond the walls of the small, sometimes crowded bookstore. They burst carefree through the building's large glass doors and strolled through wooded paths connecting classrooms and dorms. A sprawling courtyard enveloped a bubbling fountain that sprayed passersby with a fine mist on blustery days. The courtyard was encircled by a knee high, red brick wall. Beyond lay the grassy yards home to students gathering between classes—or on especially warm days, *during* classes. Frisbees and chatter filled the air. Evan and Anna reclined on the grass, prizing their newfound freedom to talk about anything and everything without fear of being overheard or interrupted. If others were near, they hardly noticed, oblivious to everything except themselves.

He followed question with question, listening intently and remembering the small things. His novel perspective and passion for learning ignited the spirit of discovery in Anna. He transformed the lifeless words of textbooks into important ideas and notable events. Anna stared at Evan while he read and explained, enamored not only with the sound of his voice, but also with its sincerity.

They rose and brushed pants, slung book bags over shoulders, and weaved through students strewn indiscriminately on the lawn. They bounced off the short brick ledge and resumed their stroll around the imposing library. They romped across a grassy square before crossing a busy intersection and hiking a short distance to the parking lot for a prolonged goodbye. They remained engrossed in conversation until Evan peeked at his watch. He was late. It happened every time.

Evan waited tables at an upscale restaurant close to campus. Generous tips supported his living expenses. But the parking lot sat slightly over a mile in the opposite direction. Every night, he sprinted across campus to his dorm room to shower and change clothes before work. He never complained. She would catch his silhouetted body running in her rearview mirror, wishing they could continue their talks into the evening.

Anna began parking in the lot furthest from campus. The closer lots were full, she assured Evan, but he was curious. She remembered the way he peered into her, and the knowing smile that followed. He knew, but he didn't press it, at least not the first few days. After a week of lengthy afternoon walks, Evan casually pointed out the empty spaces as they passed the closer lot. Anna's embarrassed grin gave her away.

With a gracious smile and eyes filled with affection, Evan leaned in close to Anna and whispered in her ear, "It's okay. I'm glad you did."

The warmth of his breath and slight touch of his lips on her ear sent tingles rippling through her body. It was the most intimate thing he had done. His daily visits and long walks confirmed his affection. But he had never said anything. Until this little whisper. *It's okay.* Something about the way he said it. He didn't want her feeling the least bit uncomfortable or self-conscious. *I'm glad you did.* Perhaps he treasured these walks as much as she.

He was disarmingly cute, she thought. Not so handsome that he thought too highly of himself. His self-deprecating humor remained refreshing. When they were together, she didn't have to pretend. She could be herself.

The intrigue grew.

When will he kiss me? Why hasn't he asked me out? Anna cherished every moment with Evan, but she wanted more. And she wanted to understand his intentions. In time, he would tell her. But not in the usual way.

The sun glared off passing cars and metal signs as Anna walked alone to her car on a late April afternoon. It never seemed this far when she walked with Evan, she thought. Anna spotted a small envelope lying diagonally under her windshield wipers. She raced across the parking lot, tearing into the envelope to find a small card.

Dear Anna,

I don't ever want to walk this far again without you by my side.

Your not-so-secret admirer,
Evan

P.S. Who happens to be admiring you right now.

Anna spun around, mouth open. There he was, smiling, eyes alive. She ran and threw herself into the solace of his arms.

She could linger there forever.

Others would have bought her candy, sent flowers. Evan surprised her. It was his way. Simple, but personal and meaningful. He expressed his affection—beautifully, intimately—in one sentence more completely than most songwriters in a three-minute ballad.

The moment signaled a turning point. Most of their dates during the previous two months had not been real dates— they had done little things together. Evan asked Anna if she would go for a ride with him after work. He planned to climb out onto the rocks overlooking Cynthiana Gorge. He teased about taking her to Lookout Point to take advantage of her, but he never did. While other college boys professed to respect her as a "friend", when given the opportunity, their actions belied their talk. Not so with Evan. Perhaps this made him all the more alluring.

Cynthiana Gorge was a lazy twenty-minute drive south of Canterbury College. Towering maples, birches and oaks vaulted over winding roads to the overlook. Sunlight flickered and danced through branches and leaves, painting a beautiful montage through their windows, as they progressed higher into the mountains. The overlook appeared on the left without notice. A cloud of dust marked their arrival at the small, unpaved lot bordered by crude log posts linked with

thick gray cable. A tranquil hush ruled the late afternoon—
the site remained a haven for locals, safe from the swarm of
tourists. A weathered sign mapped three trails, each etched
into the wood.

Evan opted for a fourth route all his own.

He bounded from his car to play the part of the southern
gentleman, pretending the mere embrace of his fair maiden's
hand unseemly. Anna feigned reluctance to take his
outstretched hand, after which he grabbed her and scurried
off. Evan's path forced a more strenuous hike through the
woods. While he claimed to appreciate the additional
exercise, Anna knew he liked holding her hand longer as
they trudged and climbed and stooped over and around
rocks. It led to a remote, yet magnificent boulder jutting out
over the canyon, where they could be alone.

Evan exuded warmth and humor with friends and
strangers alike. The way he made people feel good about
themselves reminded Anna of her grandfather. Yet he was
selfishly protective of their time alone and avoided crowds.
He loved doing everything with her. Rather than be a *part* of
his life, Evan desired her intimate involvement in everything,
from learning together to traveling to running errands.

It was a gorgeous late spring day—May twenty-seventh to
be exact, she would never forget—when Evan and Anna sat
out on *their* rock, as he called it, overlooking Cynthiana
Gorge. Converging tributaries fed by melting snow in spring
and abundant rain in autumn helped sculpt the ravine and
nourish the gushing river. Deer pranced along the banks
while a hidden kingdom of wildlife thrived under cover of
spiraling hardwoods. Soaring verdant pines pierced crystal
blue skies. Dreadful howls of gusting wind roaring through
the chasm reminded visitors the canyon was ruled by the
sovereign will of untamed nature.

Kirk Martin

Its magnificence spawned not only diverse native wildlife and flowers, it inspired Evan. On each visit, he created a story highlighting a monumental historical event shaped by the great Cynthiana Gorge. Yep, the patriots battled the redcoats in the valley below, suffering horrific casualties at the hands of the Brits before George Washington swept in to rescue the beleaguered army. Anna rested her head on his arm and listened, almost believing his tales. And sometimes she thought *he* believed them as well. He occasionally lifted her chin, saying, "Look, right over there, that's where Robert E. Lee's men broke the Union line and almost captured New England." And for a moment, his colorful prose painted pictures so clear the events unfolded before them.

Anna chuckled at absurd tales articulated with serious timbre for dramatic effect. Sure, his ancestors were fond of skinny-dipping in the frigid waters flowing through the ravine. And Elmer Fudd hunted Bugs Bunny in the dense forests below. He boasted a rather elaborate story to prove it, of course. Any strain of disbelief on her face was countered with a look of stern indignation, followed by that endearing smile.

May twenty-seventh. Like any other day. But not exactly. The gorge was vibrant in springtime. Anna tried to recall which flowers bloomed. But she remembered only one thing. She sat beside this young man awestruck, yet uncertain. She watched him speak, admiring features accentuated in sunlight, wondering if he was conscious of her stare. She loved the sparkle in his eyes, the passion in his voice and how complete she felt beside him. Her anxiety about their relationship dissolved in his words.

In the course of his story, he motioned toward the mouth of the river that formed on the western edge of the gorge. He stopped abruptly at the recognition of her stare. He was no

66

longer engaged in the story. His eyes fell from the distant sky to meet hers for what seemed an eternity. An expression different than any she had seen before played in his eyes. He bit his lip, not sure what to do with the thoughts racing through his mind. His eyes began to move across and take in her eyes, her face, her hair. She fidgeted under his gaze, unsure what he was seeing.

She spotted the faintest trace of tears as they sat in silence. He slowly moved his right hand toward her face and touched her skin, as if for the first time. She closed her eyes and breathed in the moment. When she opened her eyes, he was still gazing at her. He spoke slowly, tenderly.

"You have the face of an angel."

And at that moment Anna Matthews fell head over heels for Evan Forrester. And Evan Forrester fell in love with Anna Matthews. He had walked into a deep place inside her and opened a door she never knew existed.

He leaned in to kiss her. She could feel his body trembling, shaken by his revelation. Their lips met for the first time, slowly pressed together, in a lingering embrace. They held each other's faces and remained silent, content to let the moment last forever, their mouths touching, breath warm, intimate. Their tears intermingled, tracing the lines around their mouths and trickling from their chins to the rock below. Evan and Anna rested quietly holding each other until the sun receded in a fiery glow behind the distant mountains.

When Anna asked Evan what he had seen on the rock, he paused, then met her gaze.

"When I looked at you, I saw my best friend and my wife. I saw someone so radiant, so full of love and understanding that she could only have been sent from God's own hands."

The fury of their love caught a strong wind. Unlike most relationships fueled by intense physical attraction, only to be doused by the cooling revelation of imperfections, their affection grew steadily as they learned more about each other. Theirs had not been love at first sight—they *liked* each other long before.

The moment changed them. They became inseparable. He cut classes, surprising her in the bookstore. She sat next to him while he read and studied, his hand tracing her leg or back or arms, always touching.

Evan's stories at the Gorge matured. The bubbling streams, towering trees and picturesque valley below still formed the canvas. But the pictures changed. No longer did he speak of advancing redcoats or heroic patriots. No longer did he tell of *his* travels and adventures. Every story featured *them*.

Evan and Anna.

He had discovered something deep inside her, something that changed him. A new gravity complemented his boyish charm. He painted vivid pictures of daily life together. Not so much physical descriptions of their house and yard, but how they would interact. Turning mundane chores into events, surprising her at the grocery store, working together, sharing holidays and vacations.

Anna sat speechless. He knew her. He knew her hopes and dreams.

Sunday afternoon drives changed, too. They traveled silently for lengthy stretches, basking in a contentment spoiled by words. He chose longer routes, drove slower. Anna wrapped her arms around his and clung, nestling her head against his arm. She feared it would be uncomfortable to Evan, but if she dared lift her head or move away, he would gently beckon her closer. She took in the scent of his skin, listened to him breathe, lost herself.

◆ ◆ ◆

Anna turned the corner into the subdivision, the streets thoroughly plowed, two blocks from her house. She didn't remember the drive home. Tears stained her cheeks. David would notice. She turned around and headed to a nearby restaurant, where she could use the ladies' room and make herself more presentable for her husband. *Husband. Do I regret marrying David?*

Earlier in the day, Anna had bemoaned her predictable life. Now she sought to make sense of her discovery.

Evan Forrester made his way up the wide plank steps to the front door, pausing to glance into the clearing night sky before turning the knob, hoping by some twist of fate to catch a glimpse of a falling star. He would repeat the same wish he had uttered countless times. He stepped inside and welcomed the torrent of warm air rushing toward him. He hung his coat on the iron hook, bent to click on the lamp, and continued down the narrow hallway to the kitchen. He had not eaten since early afternoon, preferring to eat dinner after the book signing. But his stomach was disquieted. Instead, he poured a mug of warm cocoa and proceeded to the den.

French doors opened to a modest-sized room with an open, but cozy air. The room served as his sanctuary. A primitive table of hardwood pine, notched with two centuries of use, stood perpendicular to large, wood-paned windows overlooking his sloping yard. From a brown leather chair, Evan would scan the expansive Vermont countryside, his senses absorbing its splendor.

And he would write.

The desk, and the entire room, remained remarkably free of clutter. Evan preferred to write in solitude with as much open space as possible. A small wood-burning fireplace was a constant companion, the scorched brick blackened by continual use. Framed photographs capturing the magnificence of the Green Mountains hung on the walls. A picture of Middlebury Gap in autumnal brilliance graced the wall behind him, complemented by a shot of Cynthiana Gorge Evan had taken in winter, the snow lilting off the branches of proud evergreens and bare maples.

He knelt before the hearth and carefully laid a bed of tightly rolled newspaper and dry kindling beneath the heavy iron grate. Rough, splintered logs spanned above. He struck a match and watched the orange-red glow spread quickly across the papers, tiny ambers of fire spotting the thin, splintered ends of the kindling. Sparks turned to flames, drawn upward by the strong draught. The blaze held his attention as he grappled with the questions assaulting his mind. Would she call? Would they meet again?

Evan rose heavily, falling back into his chair, and turned his gaze far into the night. The faint outline of the mountains lay black against a canvas of midnight blue, lit occasionally by the moon fighting its way through drifting clouds. The crackle of the fire drew his gaze from the distant hills to the lone object on his desk beside a fountain pen and pad of paper. Evan stared at the small photograph of Anna sitting on their rock at the Gorge. She was stunning, the evening sun silhouetting her face, her eyes, her hair in a radiant glow. He felt himself being absorbed into the scene, smoke from the fire mixing with his soul's longing. The gnawing questions slowly subsided as he closed his eyes and escaped to a world where he and Anna had never parted.

Her eyes. Her beautiful green eyes. Evan could never adequately describe what he saw in Anna's eyes, but it was far deeper than the emerald apparent to others. It moved him more than the breathtaking peaks. Evan had been in love before, or so he thought, the feelings attributed mainly to physical attraction tinged with the fleeting exhilaration of youth.

But he had fallen in love with the deepest part of Anna. In her gaze, he felt accepted, wanted, needed with a completeness he had never known. It was the purest form of love. Words can be deceiving, but eyes do not lie. In Anna's eyes, Evan saw limitless horizons, where he could dream with the only person who had absolute faith in him. Faith in his tender care, that enabled Anna to give herself to him with unbridled trust. Faith in him and his dreams, even when others discounted his thoughts and derided his plans.

Evan could be himself with Anna. It sounded simple, yet in reality it was rare. Most people unconsciously impose conformity to their own preferences. Even the most sincere harbor prejudices and doubts that stifle those with a fragile internal sense. Evan needed Anna. She understood his quirks and faults, and loved more deeply. Her poise steadied his emotional whims. Her adventurous spirit shared his passion. Anna completed Evan.

The more he discovered, the more he loved her.

Evan shook himself from this thought to stoke the burgeoning fire, inviting the warmth to penetrate his soul and mend the tear inside.

Anna retreated to the bathroom, shutting the door behind her. She leaned forward, clutching the vanity to steady herself. A nauseous chill settled into her bones. She looked down and closed her eyes, attempting by sheer will to stave off the clammy, unsettled feeling. Anna worried that David knew. "Just need some sleep, honey," she had explained reassuringly. "How was your night?" she forced, trying to change the subject.

She raised her head, startled to catch her pallid reflection in the mirror. The questions continued to haunt her. Did she regret marrying David? Where had Evan been all these years? Anna splashed cool water on her face and pulled herself together. She managed to remove her make-up, brush her teeth and crawl into bed.

With a barely audible "goodnight", Anna rolled over and stared at the wall. A sliver of light slid between the blinds and cast shadows about the room. The droning of the fan in the corner helped drown out the thoughts screaming in her head. She clung to the covers pulled close to her chest.

He's out there. Thinking about me. Anna pictured him lying in bed, comforted that they were sharing this drama. *Together.* It had been a long time. And yet she felt closer to Evan in this moment than she ever had to David. This is how it had been before he left, drifting off to sleep thinking about each other.

I have been, Anna. I have been.

Evan's reply echoed through her mind before she succumbed to exhaustion. The long night had revealed one fact that remained indeterminably clear.

They had fallen in love, but they had never fallen out of love.

Chapter 9

THE SNOWSTORM threw its last flakes over western Vermont just past midnight. At daybreak, a hopeful sun chased away heavy clouds. Evan awoke, paralyzed by fear. Would she call? He set the phone's ringer to high before stepping into the shower.

The soothing heat ordinarily sparked ideas and thoughts. This morning, self-doubt and regret plagued him. None of this would have happened had he stayed home and married Anna after graduating from college.

He scrubbed shampoo into his head vigorously, trying to somehow erase history and imagine they had never separated. Preparing to graduate with a degree in American Literature, Evan had been absorbed with two immediate plans—marrying Anna and either attending graduate school or beginning his career—when another option collided squarely with his plans. As he had done repeatedly over the years, Evan questioned the decision that altered the course of his life.

Evan Forrester grew up an only child in the picturesque Vermont town of Quechee. Quechee was settled in 1764 by pioneers who established mills along the Ottauquechee River. Evan's great, great grandparents settled in the latter part of the 19th century. The Boston Red Sox and New York Yankees had donned uniforms made from the mills' quality fabric. Quechee prospered until the 1950's when the migration of affordable labor to the burgeoning South threatened Quechee's landmark mills. Dilapidated buildings with broken glass and rusted entryways spotted the once thriving village.

But the town took stock of its geological wonders. Nature had bestowed upon Quechee a landscape featuring precipitous gorges and magnificent waterfalls. As the Ice Age glaciers receded, the melting process steadily cut away the bedrock ridge that formed the spectacular Quechee Gorge, known as Vermont's Little Grand Canyon. Inspired by nature's bounty, the town transformed itself into a flourishing community of artisans and craftsmen, whose hand-made wares became widely sought.

Evan Forrester was imbued with the spirit of Quechee— infused with the curiosity of highly creative artists, lifted by the surrounding hillsides. Airy, without limitations to the east, west, south or north. On lazy summer days, Evan pedaled his bike down scenic country paths into the quiet village, dotted with antique shops and craft stores. He visited the blacksmith first. With the sound of clanking iron ringing in his ears, he raced to Simon Pearce, his favorite shop. Overlooking the covered bridge and waterfall on Ottauquechee River, Evan stood spellbound watching craftsmen create hand blown glass pieces and potters working on the wheel. Afterward, he explored the Gorge with friends, scampering along dusty trails and skipping rocks across placid water.

The climax of every summer was the Hot Air Balloon Festival. Visitors from around the globe descended upon the village to marvel at spectacular balloons painting the skies. As a toddler, Evan stood and ogled, tugging at his father's pants and pointing upward to the "ba-woons" circling high above. Evan's first excursion, at the age of fourteen, changed him. He hovered above the breathtaking Quechee Gorge and the village shops that had become his second home. The awe-inspiring beauty of sights seen previously from the ground opened new vistas. Evan Forrester learned to dream and explore the many sides of life's wonders as disparate as the seasons that brought renewal to Vermont's countryside.

But unlike the expanse around him, Evan suffered boundaries—much to his consternation. He was a PK, a preacher's kid. Mr. Forrester was actually Reverend Forrester to everyone in the small town, minister of a Methodist congregation. Mrs. Forrester served by her husband's side.

Evan endured pressures typical for a pastor's son—his actions scrutinized more closely than others, his punishment for inappropriate behavior more severe. The restrictions and expectations were stifling.

Evan wondered why his father had time for strangers and parishioners, but not his own son. The misunderstanding in his eyes pained his mother. "Your father loves you, Evan. More than you know. One day when you are older, you will realize how much. I know it's hard right now."

Not that all the memories were bad. His parents loved each other. His father took him canoeing and camping. They played baseball and soccer in the back yard. But a distance persisted. With Evan's increasing independence, their relationship grew more strained. His mother brokered the peace and provided reassurance. "You're a lot like your father, Evan, but you don't realize it. That's why you two have such difficulty."

Evan learned over time that his father struggled, occasionally overhearing his parents' conversations. His father expressed frustration at his inability to communicate with Evan and wondered whether he was a good father. On these nights, Evan slept more soundly, assured of his father's love and effort. Still, nearly every discussion ended in an argument. Perhaps they *were* too much alike.

Evan left home at eighteen to attend Canterbury College. A year later, his mother died of an aneurysm. Her death caused Evan and his father to reevaluate their relationship. While they tried to understand each other better, it suffered without her influence.

His father continued preaching at the church, but never regained his footing. He poured more time into serving people, but nothing could fill the void. Ministering without his wife only made the emptiness greater. He could not bear to stand in the pulpit and gaze into a mournful congregation. The unending sentiments of sorrow trapped him in the past. Evan's father decided to pursue a dream he had shared with his wife. They had planned to work overseas with poor children in their remaining years. Not exactly the typical Florida retirement package many of their friends were considering, but his parents had always found fulfillment in giving to others. Golf and bridge were out of the question.

Evan was not surprised when his father mentioned an opportunity to help a primitive tribe in South America. But his request for Evan's blessing humbled him. Evan recognized this service was his father's way of feeling closer to the wife he missed. In his junior year, he said goodbye to his father with newfound affection and respect. Evan continued to study hard and explore the great Vermont countryside.

In this land so open and full of wonder, his life would change.

Anna squinted at the alarm clock. Daybreak had arrived too quickly. Her eyes burned in the early morning light. The few hours of sleep provided a brief lull from the barrage of questions and images pulling her into the past. The way he nervously combed his hand through his hair, his kisses sweet with the taste of chocolate, his hand resting gently against the small of her back.

Anna completed her morning routine robotically, trying to avoid arousing David's suspicions. The shock of seeing Evan had worn off, but left in its wake a maelstrom of torn feelings. Her relationship with David, already strained, would never be the same. The inevitable comparisons to Evan promised to draw her away further. She wanted to cling to a tenderness long since forgotten. But, she remained troubled by unanswered questions.

Why had he ended their relationship? Why hadn't he contacted her after returning from South America?

On a spring day during his senior year at Canterbury, Evan had stopped by the bookstore. The ashen look on his face startled Anna. The glimmer in his eyes faded to disbelief and confusion. His eyes could not meet hers.

"What is it, Evan?"

"I got a letter from my dad today," he replied solemnly, pulling a crumpled envelope from his pocket.

"Is he okay?"

"He asked me to come help him."

Anna felt her dreams slip away. She missed Evan when they were separated for hours. She could not imagine being a continent away, not knowing when she would see him again. She felt selfish for wanting to keep Evan for herself, apart from his dad. Her reaction added to his anxiety rather than alleviating it. The subsequent wave of guilt compounded the despair.

Reverend Forrester wanted to spend time with Evan before he embarked on a career or began graduate school. Anna read the letter. "Please come, Evan," his father pleaded. The thought was unbearable, but she loved him.

They planned for Evan to be away for two years. Upon his return, they would marry and begin their life together. They spoke as if their future had been carved in stone and sanctioned by the stars. "Absence makes the heart grow fonder," they kept repeating to each other, trying to minimize the heartache.

Every night after work, Anna rushed home to search her mailbox. The perpetual stream of crossing letters mitigated the loneliness, slightly. Their letters were filled with the monotonous details of daily life, interrupted indiscriminately by expressions of affection and sorrow.

Fifteen months passed when Evan wrote that his father had contracted a grave illness. The sickness progressively worsened and his father died almost two years after Evan had arrived. Evan would be coming home, she thought. Until she received the letter.

Dearest Anna,

This is the most difficult letter I have ever written because it will be my last. I am going to stay and finish my father's work. His fingerprints shaped me into the man that you fell in love with, and I need to honor him.

I am going to stay. Those five words torment me. I may bitterly regret this decision. I may lose my best friend. I may lose the girl in whose eyes I see eternity. My greatest regret, though, would be leaving you with unending loneliness and uncertainty.

I do not know when I will return. If we continue writing, you will be unable, perhaps unwilling, to move on. And I will be unable to complete his work.

I love you. I must let you go.

The sun does not rise without tender thoughts of you. With every pass of the moon, I whisper your name into the night sky. Always.

Anna refused to believe their relationship had ended. She wrote unceasingly and ran to her mailbox daily. No reply came. Her friends eventually convinced her to begin dating again. Relationships ended quickly. But she would die inside if she did not try to get *past* Evan, though she wondered if she'd ever get *over* him. She moved to Burlington and quickly made new friends. The change of scenery and lifestyle provided a refreshing change.

A mutual friend introduced her to David. He was kind and genuine, an unusual departure from most college boys. Classic good looks, All-American boy. When he proposed, she tried not to overanalyze their relationship. She knew he'd be a faithful husband and loving father.

Uneasy thoughts occasionally gnawed at her. Though she hated to admit it, Evan was still her best friend and she'd trust him to help her decide whether to marry David. On numerous occasions, she wrote Evan, only to toss the crumpled paper in the wastebasket. Would it be fair to pull him back to her, or to tell him that she had moved on?

He had not written. He had told her to move on without him. And so she had.

At least she had tried, she thought, as she turned her attention to finish dressing. Pulling on her sweater, Anna scurried to the bathroom. She caught her reflection. Ugghh, she sighed. Her eyes were puffy and dark. She hadn't considered her appearance last night, but today was different.

Anna's hands trembled as she gripped the steering wheel. Every song spoke of lost love, so it seemed. She flipped the dial, but couldn't escape feelings from the past. The comforting ruggedness of his callused hands around her, the way he cuffed long shirt sleeves underneath, exposing his forearms—something insignificant she missed.

She rushed into the shop and dropped her coat and purse on the table. Her heart pounded. The scrap paper shook in her fidgeting hands. "Evan? Hi. It's Anna… Okay. Could you meet me for lunch at eleven-thirty at the Milton Inn in Shelburne?…Good. I'll see you then."

Just saying his name. Evan.

She was useless all morning.

Chapter 10

WHEN ANNA had last seen Evan, he was a boy. Now he was a man. The same mix of boyish charm and rugged confidence had reversed composition. He had filled out with the years, but remained lean with more definition from his labors in South America. More than his appearance, though, his manner and voice moved her. Something inside changed when he was near. When she saw him, tremendous relief washed over her, followed by a sense of peace and completeness.

Until reality made their separation clear.

As she neared the restaurant, her elation was tempered by uncertainty and fear. Anna didn't know what to expect, either of Evan or herself. She resolved to achieve closure to unanswered questions. Aware that sentiments kept unchecked would lead her astray, Anna prepared her heart. She recalled the pain he had inflicted—he had not attempted to contact her when he returned.

Pockets of snow rested atop creek stones jutting above the crests of the rushing stream. A dense thicket of trees and overgrown brush drooped over the stream's far side. The shade left its bank covered with snow, its water impenetrably dark. Evan peered down the steep incline, his feet anchored between guardrails. The rest of the brook glistened, its stones dried light brown in the sun. The Milton Inn stood perched above the gurgling water, abundant windows affording spectacular views.

Evan had arrived early. Minutes seemed like hours. A nervous perspiration left him clammy and uncomfortable. Crunching gravel drew his attention. It was Anna. His heart raced as he walked to greet her. She remained guarded. They did not hug, but instead walked awkwardly toward the restaurant. Evan held the door for her. It felt like a first date—wanting to learn about each other, but clumsy and hesitant. Evan asked for a table in the back room where they could talk privately.

The hostess led them through the restaurant, built originally as a farmhouse in the early 1800's by a prominent landowner. Masons, carpenters and other skilled craftsmen completed every detail to exacting standards. After a century as a private residence, an entrepreneur converted it to an upscale Inn in the 1920's. The downstairs comprised four separate rooms, one a kitchen, three for dining. A massive stone fireplace crackled and heated nearly the entire floor. Candles set in ornate chandeliers flickered, the melting wax forming unique molds hour after hour. The original dark plank floors remained, sloped with age, replete with character. Fine white tablecloths and linens graced elegant tables.

Sitting down, they fidgeted and glanced about, unsure how to begin. They looked at each other and half-smiled, embarrassed by their stilted behavior. A gregarious waitress broke the silence.

"Sprite?" Evan asked. Anna nodded. "Two Sprites, please."

Some things had not changed, they noticed. They wanted to break the tension, but knew it existed for their own protection. It was too soon to reminisce about their past dinners here. That time may never come.

Anna blurted out the question that had troubled her for almost a decade.

"Why did you tell me we couldn't write anymore?"

Evan paused before lifting his eyes beyond her to relive the moments. "Every night, after we worked all day and ate dinner," he began slowly, "my father and I talked for hours by firelight. We discussed my mom and college and the future." He looked at Anna with a sheepish grin. "And I talked endlessly about you."

His expression turned pensive. "When I was growing up, my father had time for everyone in the church and the community, but not for me. It seemed like his only concern was that I stay out of trouble and uphold the family name. In South America, for the first time, he listened."

Anna leaned forward, watching him intently. Evan fidgeted with his napkin and recalled a conversation. "My father said, 'Evan, your mom was right. We are a lot alike. And maybe that's why we didn't get along so well. I'm sorry I haven't been a better father. You don't know how much it means to me that you came.'

"My father worked tirelessly. The people loved him, Anna. He would cradle sick children and weep when they died. I asked him how he could care so tenderly for strangers. He looked at me and said, 'Every time I hold a child in my arms, I see you.'" Evan looked out the window, blinking away tears.

"He taught them how to read and write, how to irrigate and grow food. He taught them there was a God who cared about them. And they believed. Because they saw how he cared for them.

"I never understood my father until I saw him with the people in that village. He was a broken man after my mom's death, but a strong man. I began to see the good things in my dad and realized that I inherited many of his qualities. We just had passion for different things. It's hard to explain, Anna."

The protective walls she had tried to construct were no match, her heart rendered defenseless by his sincerity and gentleness. He stuttered occasionally, frustrated by his inability to express his feelings. But he wanted to share his deepest thoughts—who could not cherish that quality in a man? Someone so assured, so trusting of her love, that after nearly eight years apart, he would bare his soul to her.

He had not changed. She was glad.

And as he spoke, she lost herself in his world—no, *their* world—clinging to the very connection she had resolved to withstand.

"I lived the first twenty years of my life practically apart from my father. But after I spent time with him, I realized how much we meant to each other. He was no longer my father—he became my dad. When his sickness worsened, I took on most of the responsibilities so he could rest. We tried to fill every moment together, talking late into the night.

"He always thought he would die in his sleep. Every night, as he was drifting off, he would mutter, 'Goodnight, Evan. I love you, son.' Other people take that for granted. I looked forward to that all day."

Evan was there again. Anna could see it in his eyes. He was with his Dad. She was a mere bystander.

"My dad would look at me while we were working and ask, 'What are you thinking about?' And I'd keep working and reply, 'Nothing.' And he'd say, 'Evan, I know that look. Who do you think you got it from?' I could hear the smile on his face. Then he'd say, 'She must be very special.' And all I could ever say was, 'She is, Dad. She really is.'"

Evan looked away again. Exhaling, he apologized before continuing.

"I remember describing you. We were digging trench lines and talking about that day at the Gorge, out on the rock. I told him that when I looked up at you, I saw the face of an angel. That I thought God sent you to me from His own hands. Dad had his back to me, but I could hear him sniffling and see tears falling to the ground, and I knew he was thinking about Mom.

"A few months later he died. I had waited so long to see you. I began packing my belongings and found a note scratched on an old piece of paper. All it said was, 'Evan, I am proud that you are my son. I love you. Dad.' I watched the people come by and honor him—how much they wept at his passing—and I knew that I had to stay and finish what he started.

"I needed to complete his passion before I pursued mine. I had no idea how long it would take—maybe three years or more—but I couldn't ask you to wait. And I knew I couldn't complete it if I kept writing to you because my heart would be torn. That's when I wrote the letter. I know it doesn't make sense. I agonize over that decision every day, Anna, but it seemed like the right thing to do at the time. I hoped that one day you would be able to forgive me."

Anna instinctively reached across the table. "I do, Evan. I do. But I would have…"

Evan didn't let her finish. "You know, he never asked me to stay. He told me he wanted me to go home as soon as he died. He said, 'Go get your...'"

He breathed deeply, audibly, trying to collect himself. "My Dad used to call you my 'angel'. He would say, 'Go home and get your angel before she flies away.'"

The sight of Evan holding back tears for his father—or were they for her as well?—made them flow more freely down Anna's cheeks.

"I guess I found my father, but I lost my angel."

Anna watched the boy she had fallen in love with, now a grown man, sob. He was weeping for his father and he was weeping for her. He looked up, his eyes swollen.

"I'm sorry, Anna. I know..."

"Evan, it's okay. I understand," she reassured.

They sat, in tearful silence, again self-conscious.

"I need a minute. Will you excuse me?"

Anna rose, walking quickly toward the bathroom, dabbing her eyes with a tissue. She wasn't concerned about her appearance. She needed a break from the intensity. A chance to regain control of her emotions. God, it would be so easy to resume the relationship, she thought. But she still had questions. Don't let yourself fall, she kept repeating, as she made her way to the far side of the restaurant.

Evan combed through the thoughts in his head, unsure if he had answered everything to Anna's satisfaction, but aware that the tension had dissipated. He ordered another soda to wash away the sour taste in his mouth. He stared blankly through panes of glass framed with fragile drapes of ice. Icicles swollen with winter relinquished their hold to the bright January sun one drop at a time. The mercury had risen well above freezing—a welcome respite, but one that would be long forgotten when the frigid Alberta gusts returned.

Lost in the rhythmic patter of drops reluctantly falling one after another, gradually widening the circle of receding snow below, Evan remembered his return.

His stomach knotted as the plane skidded down the runway in Boston. He had waited five years to see Anna. He could not envision life without her. And now he pursued her, hoping against the odds that she had stayed single or waited for him. As he exited the plane and hiked up the ramp, the force of desire and longing overpowered reason and logic. He searched for Anna amongst the sea of travelers.

Of course she wouldn't be there waiting for him. How could she? She hadn't heard from him in years.

Mothers and daughters embraced, fathers tossed toddlers in the air and couples walked hand-in-hand. The orderly chaos stood in stark contrast to the remote village where he spent his adult life. He acclimated himself to the unwritten rules of rushing crowds. He dragged suitcases to a long rental car line, his former impatience replaced by a serene appreciation of all that surrounded him. Rather than board a connecting flight into Burlington, Evan had decided to make the trip by car. He missed driving. Absorbing the familiar countryside would enable an easier adjustment to his new life. But as he entered the freeway, its myriad green signs pointing to various destinations, a thought struck Evan.

No one was waiting for him. No one expected his arrival.

He had no one to come home to. Not his mom. Nor his dad. Not even Anna.

No one.

The thought panicked Evan. The people of the village had become his family.

He would find his boyhood home in Quechee empty.

Evan shook himself from the thought, stirred by the rugged humility of the towering pines and green mountains.

87

He reminisced until the receding sun cast a portrait of color in the evening clouds.

Evan pulled to a stop in the driveway. He rested his hands on the steering wheel and leaned forward, staring at the big house. Loneliness stared back. He lugged bulging suitcases to the front door, dropping them to the splintered porch to dig through his pockets. The doorknob wiggled as he turned the key. He opened the door and stepped into a tall foyer. The hair on his arms bristled at the musty, cold draft sweeping down the stairway. He reached for the light switch, but the dark persisted. The wind slammed the door shut behind him. He strolled through each room.

A house filled with memories. A house empty without family.

He had to see Anna. Her last letter bore a Burlington postmark. His instincts told him to check the yellow pages for a craft store in Burlington with a familiar name. He found it, he thought, on a sloping street overlooking Lake Champlain. "Angel's Wings." He would see Anna in the morning.

Food held no allure, sleep eluded him. Sheets and pillows became a tangled mess. Had she waited for him?

Evan's hand fumbled through blackness to silence the alarm. He sprang from bed with restless energy. His eyes winced at the bathroom light. He showered and skipped breakfast, leaving early for the ninety-minute drive to Burlington. As the sun peeked above the horizon, he exited the highway and wound through light downtown traffic. Perspiration beaded on his palms. An exhilarating rush engulfed him. Parking three blocks away, Evan scrambled from his car and covered the distance to the center of town swiftly.

Evan absorbed the morning. The ripple of the breeze brushing his skin, the amber sun reflecting softly off Lake Champlain, leaves rustling across dry pavement, the aroma of pancakes wafting through town. He camped in the alcove of an unopened store, surveying the downtown market. Cars rolled past. Women and men in business attire rushed by.

He glanced repeatedly at his watch, willing the hands to move faster. Close to 7:30. Still no sight of Anna. Ten minutes later. Nothing. He shifted and fidgeted. 7:45. Where is she? Now 7:55. From behind a bus she emerged. Eternity could not prepare him for this moment. He had to think to breathe. His eyes welled up, his mouth parched, able only to whisper her name. "Anna. My Anna."

Their dreams—the wedding, children, growing old together—thrust him from the storefront. His head throbbed. His heart pounded. His steps quickened. She turned the corner. He lost her. Panic. He weaved in and out, peering above the crowd. A crowd unaware of the drama unfolding.

Her energy drew him. Anna would look at him in astonishment, tears streaming. She would collapse into his strength, oblivious to the world, his voice her consolation. Her eyes would search for answers. When did you get back? Why haven't you written? He would quiet her lips, whispering, "Everything's okay now. We're together."

There she is again. Less than fifty feet away. He squeezed through the crowd, brushing elbows and shoulders, his eyes fixed, gaining ground. Almost there. Desperation and hope coursing through his body. His breath caught in his chest.

She turned her head. She must know that I am close, he thought. Her eyes. He caught a glimmer of her green eyes. He was about to call out her name, his mouth beginning to form the word Anna, when his world stopped.

Her lips met the lips of another man.

"Evan?"

Startled, he glanced up at Anna, trying to erase the haunting image.

"Are you okay?" She had regained her composure, at least on the outside.

"Uh huh. Yeah, I'm fine." The memories of that moment collided with reality. Now as then, he beheld the woman he adored. But she belonged to someone else.

A fresh Sprite fizzed in front of him. He hadn't noticed the waitress.

"Evan," she began softly, "can I ask you another question?" She remained hesitant, afraid that the answer—like the previous one—would further dismantle her defenses. She wanted to assume the worst—that he had callously disregarded her after returning—and pry any vestiges of affection from her heart while she could.

Responding to his nod, Anna continued. "Why didn't you contact me when you came back?"

Evan shifted in his seat and grimaced. He began to recount the story. He spoke in a slow, even tone, trying to quell the emotion. She would have been justified to question why he thought there was even a remote chance she would be waiting for him. But she sat motionless, immersed in him, awed by the innocent passion with which he pursued her.

He struggled to speak above the rising din of the pressing lunchtime crowd. He returned his eyes to catch her gaze.

"I saw you, Anna. For the first time in five years. You were so graceful and radiant. I lost my breath. It was like I was in a dream, and I had to catch my angel before she flew away." Evan paused and glanced away for a moment. "But I was too late, Anna. Our dream ended."

The weight of his words and the pain in his eyes devastated her. No amount of regret could change the past.

The man sitting across the table loved her more than anyone ever could.

Chapter 11

EVAN DASHED up the basement stairs to grab the phone. It was Anna. Thank God.

"I need to run to Manchester next Tuesday to buy supplies and select new fabrics. I was wondering if you'd like to ride along."

"Yeah, I'd love to, Anna," Evan replied, trying to temper his enthusiasm.

"I can't promise it will be exciting. I'll be with suppliers part of the day."

"That will be fine. I love Manchester. Really. You know me. I can always find something to do." Evan discerned a subtle change in Anna's voice. More relaxed, comfortable.

"Well, I thought we could use the time to talk. But, really, if you don't want to or can't go, you don't…"

"I want to, Anna."

"I'll call you on Monday then."

"Okay. Have a good weekend."

Talk. What did she mean? Her voice seemed warmer. But what about her relationship with her husband? He had lingering questions. Questions he feared asking.

They were both drained and needed time to put their new relationship in perspective. The realization that she had not thought about David in days—not even missed him—shocked her. How could she overlook her husband, as if he were a stranger? But she could not escape the draw of her every thought to Evan. She wondered where he lived, what his life was like, what he was doing at each moment. She wondered if he, too, was consumed with thoughts of her.

Each January, Anna met with suppliers and experts throughout New England to understand trends in fashion, furniture and design. She incorporated the fabrics, colors and styles into her gift and keepsake creations. The timing couldn't have been better. Anna usually traveled while shop traffic waned and tax season inundated David.

Manchester rested in the heart of Vermont, one hundred miles south of Burlington. The trip took about two and a half hours over winding Route 7, passing meandering brooks, brushing against the fringes of the Green Mountain National Forest. Anna suggested they meet in Middlebury and ride together for the remaining hour, making it more convenient for Evan. But he insisted on picking her up in Burlington so they could have more time together. She happily obliged.

Driving north through the Champlain Valley, the purity of the pristine blanket held Evan's gaze—something about the way the boundless snow shimmered in the sun. Adorning lofty evergreens and clothing the naked branches of white birches, forming drifts along pitched roofs, contrasting with the red outline of distant barns and trimming the edges of road signs.

The countryside's breathtaking simplicity eased the familiar rush of anxious anticipation. Evan knew the future promised nothing, but he determined to savor every moment with Anna.

He parked his Explorer in the empty lot facing north and waited. Cars and trucks and buses zipped past. Identifying Anna's car, he brushed his hand through his hair and cleared his throat before hopping out of the truck.

The crisp morning breeze swept her hair back, the sun reflecting a beauty he had missed. She was altogether lovely.

"Hi, Anna!"

"Hey, Evan! How are you? It's a beautiful day for a trip."

Their faces were beaming.

Evan held the passenger door open as Anna climbed in. "All in?" he asked. Anna looked down and pulled her coat tight. His eyes remained fixed on her as he closed the door with both hands. She welcomed Evan's gaze, smiling into his eyes. Scampering around the truck, Evan took a deep breath in a vain attempt to control his elation, his infatuation obvious.

Although they had been apart for many years, they sat quietly as Evan pulled out onto Route 7. They could not interrupt their smiles long enough to begin conversation. After exchanging embarrassed glances, Evan broke the silence and asked Anna about her business. She told him how she acquired the property and how much she enjoyed her shop. Anna quickly realized one of the reasons she missed Evan—she didn't need to explain everything to him. He understood what she meant—not just the literal meaning—but the deeper significance.

For the next two hours, they lost themselves in conversation. About her business and her family, movies they had seen, mostly trivial things made more interesting by his perspective. They interrupted each other only to appreciate breathtaking sights or deer leaping in the distance. They reminisced and giggled freely.

Occasionally, they drove past landmarks or recalled topics that evoked intimate memories. Each retreated for a moment, preferring to relive these moments in their own minds. They intended to enjoy a carefree day, not entangled with the pressure of circumstances.

They passed a pond, frozen over with traces of snow lingering between figure eight patterns scribbled atop the surface. A mother and small boy—face hidden behind coat, scarf, hat and mittens—skated hand-in-hand across the ice. The boy made small chopping steps while his mother patiently steadied him. Evan remembered the first time he skated with Anna. He had invited her to a Friday night pond skate in his hometown. Families and friends gathered, roasting hot dogs and marshmallows over blazing bonfires, as much to keep warm as to dispel hunger.

He and Anna circled the pond, reveling in each other. Her hair would catch the breeze, revealing green eyes and golden skin reflecting the glow of the fire and moon. Evan shoved his gloves into coat pockets, hands bitten by the raw chill before reaching for Anna's hand. Their fingers entwined tightly. They skated until their feet ached, unwilling to let go of each other—and the magic of the moment.

Evan glanced over, taken with long curls spiraling along her ears, the way her hair wisped around her face in waves, soft and full of life. Playful, innocent. She had not changed.

They wound through the majestic Battenkill Valley under the watchful shadow of Mt. Equinox. Its 3,800-foot high peaks towered over Manchester. Skiers from nearby Stratton and Bromley mountains would descend from the slopes in the evening to enjoy fine dining, theater or dance. Far more than a vibrant village of upscale designer outlets, the town boasted a rich heritage to complement its New England charm.

Plans to finance Vermont's role in the Revolution by confiscating Tory estates originated in Manchester. Mrs. Abraham Lincoln and Mrs. Ulysses S. Grant spent summers in the town. Robert Todd Lincoln, son of President Lincoln, made his home in Manchester. His estate, Hildene, remained a beautifully preserved destination for visitors.

Evan drove slowly along the elm-lined streets, dotted with art galleries, bookstores and restaurants. He stopped in front of a restored colonial for Anna's first appointment. They agreed to meet for lunch in an hour.

The noontime crowds dispersed from the streets as the clock struck one. Anna strolled to the Chantilly Inn, searching for Evan. The Chantilly Inn was a charming café, decidedly bright and open. Small tables with pretty tablecloths and fresh flowers were spaced well apart. Holiday trimmings remained on windows, adding cheer and color throughout the long winter.

Evan appeared. "So what took you so long?" he asked playfully.

"What do you mean? I was only gone for an hour."

"No way, you were gone for hours, Anna! Look, it's almost one o'clock," he said, tapping his watch.

"And what time did I leave, Evan? It was noon, remember?"

"Well," he said softly, "it sure seemed like hours to me."

A hostess led them to their table before the moment turned awkward. "Enjoy your meal," she said pleasantly, placing menus before them. Anna opened hers and appeared puzzled. A handwritten note obscured the daily specials. Glancing up, she caught Evan peeking above his menu. She looked back down and read.

I left you in the morning,
And in the morning glow,
You walked a way beside me
To make me sad to go.
Do you know me in the gloaming,
Gaunt and dusty gray with roaming?
Are you dumb because you know me not,
Or dumb because you know?

All for me and not a question
For the faded flowers gay
That could take me from beside you
For the ages of a day?
They are yours, and be the measure
Of their worth for you to treasure,
The measure of the little while
That I've been long away.

The revealing words were not lost on her. She gazed at
Evan, wanting to touch his skin and feel the warmth of his
lips. "I can't remember the last time I read Robert Frost.
Thank you, Evan. It's beautiful."

"I hoped you would like it. I was wandering around town
and ended up in Northshire Bookstore—imagine that." He
smiled at his own predictability. "I lost myself in some books
and remembered how we enjoyed the Robert Frost Trail. I
thought *Flower-Gathering* was perfect for today."

"It was. And is."

Their eyes lingered in thick silence.

Their hands crept tentatively across the table, tingling
with the anticipation of touching, when the waitress set water
before them.

"So what sounds good to you today?" Evan asked. He paused for a moment, surveying the menu. "I think everything is good, although the selection is limited. Do you see the PB&J anywhere?"

Anna laughed out loud. "Still?" she questioned with a hint of genuine astonishment.

"Oh yeah!" Evan replied with an unabashed grin. Anna had always made fun of his fondness for peanut butter and jelly sandwiches. Now he was in his thirties and apparently hadn't outgrown this strange predilection toward what she deemed kids' food.

They ordered soup and sandwiches and resumed their conversation. Anna shared how the knowledge from the supplier would impact her planning. Pausing abruptly, Anna studied the surrounding tables.

"What's wrong, Anna?"

"Nothing," she said with longing resignation. She wanted to give in, but she couldn't. At least not yet.

"What is it then?" He tried to hide the slight upturn of his lips.

"How did you remember?"

"Remember what?" He asked with not-so-convincing innocence.

"My favorite flowers! Every other table has pink roses. Ours is the only one with daisies. You did that, didn't you?"

"I don't know what you are talking about." The smile that charmed her as a young woman melted her.

"You are too much."

"I think the wine is getting to you, is what I think. You know, that stuff will mess with your head if you don't watch it," he kidded, raising his glass for a long sip to hide his smile.

It was Evan. Do something sweet and thoughtful, downplay it and end with a joke. And that smile. He had not changed, either.

The hour passed too quickly. Anna had an afternoon appointment with another supplier. "Now you be good this time," she admonished.

She turned the corner, arms swinging, a bounce in her step. This is what love felt like.

The late afternoon sun was soon swallowed by the graying winter sky. Time to head back to Burlington. Evan drove slowly, allowing others to pass. Had circumstances been different, they could have picked up where they had left off eight years ago. So natural. Talking effortlessly and laughing easily. It was *them* again. She could think of only one word to describe it.

Blissful.

"So was it a productive day?" Evan asked.

"Very. Discovered some design trends that will help me plan this year."

"Good. I'm glad it was worth it."

"It was." She paused and looked at Evan. "Definitely."

"So tell me about your nieces and nephews."

They eased into conversation again, eager to fill in the missing pieces of their lives. Evan admired Anna as she spoke, the painted sky beyond forming the perfect backdrop. Her face still shone. Neither the lines of worry nor the ravages of time had sullied her countenance. He saw her beauty in varied hues—how she spoke of family, the passion for her business, unassuming glances, her laugh. Not to mention a figure pleasantly accentuated with curves.

Here

"Hey!" Anna screamed, flailing in her seat and gripping her door handle. "Evan, what are you doing?!"

The truck fishtailed into a Dairy Queen parking lot.

"Stopping for an ice cream, of course!"

"Evan, it's freezing out!"

"Freeze schmeeze. It's the perfect time. It won't melt. Besides, I haven't had an ice cream cone since, well, probably since, you know. Come on, Anna."

They jumped out of the truck and raced into the store, buzzing with teenage banter. Anna excused herself to visit the ladies' room. Evan studied the flavors, searching huge frozen drums on opposite ends of the counter.

Anna weaved through kids and backpacks sprawled between tables, smiling at Evan as she returned. He handed her a cone and napkin.

"You know what? I'm sorry, Anna. I didn't even think about it. It was just like when we..."

"I know, Evan. It's fine. Really."

"Still your favorite?" he asked hopefully.

"Still."

They smiled above large scoops, huddled close over a small table, knees brushing. Oblivious to the restless commotion around them.

Anna peered into eyes that knew her. She realized Evan had never experienced life apart from her. She was all he ever had.

"Hey, watch it, Mister!" Anna warned playfully. Evan had pelted her with a snowball on the way to the truck.

"Come on. Let's see that arm, Anna."

"You're going to regret this. Remember, I was trained by two older brothers. Better run for cover." Anna bent down and tightly packed the snow in her hands. She raised her arm to hurl the snowball.

"But you still throw like a girl," Evan teased.

"Hey, what's that supposed to mean?" she asked indignantly.

Anna chased Evan, knowing—or at least hoping—that he would not dare throw a snowball at close range. He was laughing too hard to run fast. She caught him, giggling while shoving snow down the back of his jacket.

"Okay, I'll give you until ten to get back to the truck before I nail you again. One. Two. Ten!" he roared before sprinting after her. Evan caught Anna as she scooted around the front of the truck for cover. He grabbed her from behind, his arms wrapped around her waist. They bent over and gasped for air, breathless more from giggling than romping in the snow. Their lips were close. Their eyes held each other. They reveled in the tension for a moment.

"Better be getting back, huh?" Evan offered.

As day gave way to evening, they settled comfortably into the warm truck. They stared out their windows. Barns and farmhouses dotting the countryside became gray silhouettes against an infinite landscape. High, wafting clouds painted pink and red and purple streaked in loosely formed wisps across the heavens as if created by the stroke of a painter's brush. Smoke from chimneys drifted upward as the moon and stars began their dance in the evening sky.

They were content, absorbing each moment, alive and renewed. The truck had become their refuge, the settling darkness insulating them from the outside world.

Anna reflected on their day. The poem. The daisies. The way he kidded her about taking so long, subtly letting her know he missed her. It all came back. The things he said and did that stunned her with their sweetness. Tender.

Thoughtful. Anna snuck peeks of him as he drove. There was an air of something about him, an energy that drew her. Partly his voice, his laugh, and the funny things he said and did, but also the sincerity and warmth that flowed from him. All of it combined to create an incredibly alluring man. An allure that was arousing mentally, emotionally and physically.

"Evan," she began softly, "last week at the college, I asked you why you had never written to me. And you said, 'I have been.' What did you mean?"

A slight sigh escaped him. His eyes became glassy, soft, tender.

"Anna, the books…the books are my love letters to you."

Anna sidled up next to him, their bodies touching for the first time. She slipped her arm through his, clutching his forearm. She pressed her head against his arm and held tight. The way she used to. Evan's arm melted into her touch. He kept his gaze forward, not wanting this moment to pass.

"I never had plans for a future apart from you. I don't believe our love ever ended. We just never had a chance to complete it. I would stay up all night and write letters and poems expressing my love for you—how much I missed you and how empty I was without you—but I thought you would resent me if I interrupted your marriage. So I didn't mail them. But I was still deeply in love with you, Anna. And I needed to tell you."

Anna pressed harder. Evan leaned his body into her and spoke softly.

"My dad told me he could never love another woman besides my mom. He went to South America to fulfill their dream. I write the novels so we can share our dreams. They aren't written for anyone else, Anna. Just you."

Anna absorbed every word, every feeling, his consuming devotion. They rode in silence the rest of the way home. She wept quietly on Evan's arm, grasping him tighter, not wanting to let go of this man. Ever. He had walked inside her again and occupied that deep place. She wanted him to stay.

Anna ran through the garage to a small laundry room. She kicked her shoes off, clicked on the lights and continued through the kitchen, flinging her purse to the counter and shedding her coat over a waiting chair. She ignored the flashing red light on the answering machine and rushed down the narrow hallway to the foyer, turning up the stairs. Running into the master bedroom, she grabbed the book from the nightstand, her fingers fumbling to find the dedication.

Every page whispers your name.
Anna surrendered.

Chapter 12

FIERY ORANGE specks dotted the splintered kindling. Evan knelt, placing dried logs split the previous fall across the iron grate. Hearing the crowd, he leaned back to catch the instant replay. He closed the screen and returned to the leather sofa, opening a beer and propping his feet on the antique trunk.

Watching college basketball on cold winter nights with his father remained a fond childhood memory. The passage of time changed Evan's perspective—his father had spent more time with him than he had thought. He couldn't recall when the tradition started—it had evolved into a weekly event. His mother always seemed to have plans on those nights, leaving Evan and his father alone. They sat by the fire and snacked on pizza, chips and soda late into the night. Might as well have been prime rib. He cheered for the same teams as his father, and that had not changed.

Sentimental thoughts mingled with the euphoria of spending the day with Anna. He felt the light, warm impress of her head on his arm. Deep, tender, intimate. The soft strands of her hair tracing his neck.

◆◆◆

David's reflection in the bathroom mirror startled Anna.

"You scared me," she said, already spent and on edge.

"I'm sorry, honey." David moved closer to deliver a playful kiss. Anna offered her cheek.

The situation remained surreal to her. David had come home, expecting a normal night, unaware of what she had experienced. They were in two different worlds, worlds which were colliding.

She was still with Evan.

"Why are you so late?" she asked, diverting attention.

"Didn't you get my message? I told you I would be working late." David's eyes narrowed. "You okay?"

With a feeble nod, Anna spun around and switched the blow dryer on high. David backed off and walked to his closet to change clothes. She stared in the mirror, but saw nothing. She didn't want to be standing in this bathroom, in this house, with this man. She did not want to talk, did not want to touch. She wanted to keep her day with Evan sacred.

She sat silently through dinner, occasionally mumbling between David's work stories. Her expression remained blank, indifferent. David was a stranger, an intruder.

She was listening to Evan speak gently of his love for her. Her fingers were stroking the soft, dark hair on his forearms. She breathed in the musky scent of his skin each time she drew the fork to her mouth.

An American flag flew stiffly in the February wind, flapping proudly above Evan as he passed the small post office. The frigid morning air penetrated his lungs. He walked briskly into town, arms held close, hands buried in his winter jacket. Jeans, a heavy rugby and hiking boots kept him warm most days while he breathed in the fresh New England air. Today, though, he felt like the parked cars lining the streets—frozen solid by a hard overnight freeze. Evan listened to the sounds of a winter morning. Engines whirring and whining back to life. Windshields scraped clear with frantic thrusts, ice shavings at the whim of bitter gusts. People cursed without the shelter of a garage no doubt welcomed spring. No matter the season, Evan's routine remained the same. Rise with the sun and walk the mile into town for a morning paper and necessities from Dennison's Grocery. He preferred the exercise to driving or having his paper delivered.

Evan passed a small dairy farm and open land before reaching a residential neighborhood. Tree-lined streets and familiar sidewalks kept him company amidst the historic colonials, many of which dated from the 1770's. A traditional red saltbox, partially hidden by impressive maples, served as a signpost that the town stretched beyond. Evan gazed at the saltbox, wondering if revolutionary figures had lived there, imagining the rich history of its owners and guests over three centuries. Just past the home, a sloping street dove into the village. Small shops rested one after another in almost perfect symmetry. Striking verdant pines spiraled above snow-drenched hills surrounding the town. Evan never ceased to be awestruck by the glory of the orange sun emerging above the peaks.

He strolled across the arching footbridge overlooking Otter Creek. Its falls hummed the same song morning, noon and night. Evan scampered through an opening in the walls of snow piled high before crossing the street. He hopped the curb and entered the small grocery store.

"Well, hello there, Evan," chirped the old man. Henry Dennison was in his seventies—or so everyone thought. No one knew for sure. Henry wore his usual khaki pants, creases worn away years before, and a dated plaid dress shirt—

absent the top button—beneath a soiled blue apron. If you strained, you could make out the faded store name printed on the apron. The store had stayed pretty much the same since his father had opened it, with an old-fashioned cash register and stickered prices on every product.

"Good morning, Mr. Dennison."

"Beautiful morning out there, isn't it?" The shopkeeper's greeting was the same whether sun, rain or snow ruled the day.

"Sure is. How are you today, sir?"

"Can't complain, son, can't complain. Besides," he chuckled, amused at his own statement, "wouldn't do me any good, now, would it?" He stretched his neck forward and peered into Evan's eyes.

"I suppose not," Evan replied, continuing down the narrow aisles. The hollow look in the old man's eyes would not release him. Evan turned around and stepped toward Mr. Dennison. "I hear a big snowstorm is on the way."

This was Mr. Dennison's cue to repeat the forecast. He told Evan when the storm would arrive, its duration and the predicted accumulation. Evan listened patiently as he described past snowstorms in great detail. He had heard these stories countless times.

The conversation moved to sports. Most of the locals, including Mr. Dennison, had adopted Boston franchises as their own. Whether it was the Red Sox, Patriots, Celtics or Bruins, Henry Dennison repeated the familiar mantra. "I think this is going to be their year." Decades had passed since his prediction proved true.

"I heard the Sox are reporting for training camp in a few weeks," Evan offered, sparking further conversation.

"Yes, sir, and they have quite a team coming back this year..." Mr. Dennison mentioned every player, weaving in stories of past heroes. He could talk about the Sox for fifteen minutes without taking a breath. And so it was every morning.

Henry Dennison didn't operate the grocery store to make money. It was all he had left. And the only way he could be assured of conversation each day. Evan walked into town every morning—not only for fresh air and exercise, but because he recognized the loneliness in the old man's eyes. He had seen it in his dad's eyes.

He saw it in the mirror everyday.

Mrs. Dennison had been at her husband's side every day for forty years. Seeing the couple together remained an enduring image for most people in town. They teased each other and bickered in front of customers. But everyone knew it was an act. They were made for each other and never took it for granted. Mrs. D—as she liked to be called—passed away five years earlier, leaving Mr. Dennison to care for the store. Like Evan's father, he had lost his best friend.

When Evan first frequented the store, he would walk away shaking his head, weary of Mr. Dennison's senseless babble and rote conversations. Until he remembered his father.

Every time I hold a child in my arms, I see you.

From that moment, when Evan greeted Mr. Dennison, he saw his own father. He understood the piercing loneliness. Whenever he stood with groceries in hand—his frozen food melting or an important task waiting at home—Evan remembered his dad. And he stood and listened patiently to the old man talk. The same reason he tried to make it into town later in the afternoon.

With a mix of genuine reluctance and relief, Evan tried to wrap up the conversation. "I better be going, Mr. Dennison."

"Okay, son, you come back soon."

"I will." He gave Mr. Dennison a friendly pat on the arm, looking warmly into his eyes. "You have a good day, Mr. Dennison."

Evan bundled up and retraced his path, muttering a prayer under his breath for Mr. Dennison. Nothing in particular, just asking for a comforting hand to rest on a lonely man.

Passing by the old saltbox, Evan's thoughts returned to Anna. Their worlds had been turned upside down. Years ago, he had reconciled that they would never be together. Now it seemed possible. Feelings confined to their own hearts for a decade flooded out like water released from a dam. Where would it lead? He feared creating false hopes. He feared having his heart shattered again.

He wanted to know why she married David, but he hadn't asked. It wouldn't be fair. He had implored her to move on. Still, Evan sensed something awry. They had talked at length about her shop and her family, but never about David. He thought he had seen traces of regret in her eyes the first time she acknowledged her marriage. Or maybe he only *hoped* for trouble between Anna and David.

Susan burst through the shop door carrying a large, handled bag from The Mountain Deli. Anna needed an objective friend to help sort through her thoughts. They had spoken at length about Evan since their meeting at the book signing, but Susan encouraged her to be strong and maintain her perspective. She was skeptical of Evan's return and questioned his intentions. Why did he break off the relationship? Why didn't he try to find you when he came back? He probably met someone else. When that didn't work out, he sought you, Anna. You are in love with the past, with memories from carefree days. Who doesn't reminisce with fondness? Susan repeated the logical reasons Anna should stay with David and why she should be happy. Anna didn't disagree with anything Susan said—her arguments made sense. But Susan couldn't understand the connection Anna and Evan shared. She had never experienced anything even close. Susan's perspective was colored by a series of shallow relationships with selfish men.

"So what's up, kiddo?" Susan asked.

"Evan and I spent the day together yesterday and..."

"And? Did you find out why he never came back for you?" Susan asked sharply. Her words had stung. "I'm sorry, Anna. I didn't mean to be so blunt and..."

"It's okay," Anna replied. "But to answer your question, yes, I did find out."

Anna explained Evan's reasons for going to South America. Susan interrupted. "Yeah, I know all that, but why didn't he come back to get you?"

"I'll get to that. If you'll let me finish." Susan recoiled with the tone. Anna recounted how Evan had reconciled with his father. He had stayed to honor his father and the people who loved him. Susan's countenance began to soften.

"When did he come back?"

"Four years ago. He came back to find me." Anna retold the complete story, her voice resonating with affection for Evan, grieving her loss. "Susan, he was that close. A few steps away. And then he saw me kiss David."

"Oh, God, Anna." Susan tried to resist her growing warmth toward Evan. "But if he wanted to be with you, why didn't he write or contact you?"

Anna placed the book in front of Susan.

Shuffling across the hardwood floors still half asleep and half frozen, Kelli peered through squinted eyes at the sun greeting the frost-laden yard. She reached into the cupboard for her morning salvation. A small envelope fell into her hand. A wide smile chased away any vestiges of weariness.

Through shades of blue and founts so sweet
I looked o'er blooms til glances should meet.

The day my eyes beheld you, I was born
Every minute apart leaves me bare, forlorn.

My heart did prance and skip a beat
When I found in you I was complete.

Never let me go, not from your sight
Lest I lose my way, my hope, my light.

If heaven intend just one, then I know 'tis you
Eyes, lips, breath tell me it is true.

Come, run with me, my bride, my friend
Let us not stop, breathless, love hath no end.

Happy Anniversary, Kelli! It's been eight years, seven months and twenty-three days, but it seems like yesterday. I couldn't wait another four months and seven days to tell you how happy I am to be your husband.

I adore you, sweet girl.
Justin

P.S. In case you couldn't tell from my poem…you may want to pack some clothes for the weekend. Think sunshine and sand. I'll be home for you at noon.

Susan looked up. "This is very sweet, Anna, but what does it have to do with you?"

Anna leafed back to the dedication.

Every page whispers your name.

Susan looked up, puzzled.

"Susan, Evan wrote this to me. For me. These books are his love letters to me. They tell *our* story."

Susan's mouth dropped. She remained speechless, contemplating the meaning.

Anna continued. "That's what the dedication means: every page whispers your name. He was speaking to me through the novels. That's why I felt the connection to the characters and the books."

"Oh, my God, Anna! If you could do whatever you wanted, what would you do?"

"Be with Evan."

The answer came so quickly it surprised even Anna.

Dark, loosely formed clouds—the harbinger of the coming storm—hung in the distance. Pen in hand, Evan turned his gaze to the empty pad below. The paper had stared blankly at him for weeks. He had no new story to write. He was experiencing it.

Tossing his pen aside, Evan marched to the living room. He picked the collection of Robert Frost poems off the chest, perusing the pages while slowly returning to the comfort of his den. He never failed to find new meaning in the poems.

The birds have less to say for themselves
In the wood-world's torn despair
Than now these numberless years the elves,
Although they are no less there:
All song of the woods is crushed like some
Wild, earily shattered rose.
Come, be my love in the wet woods, come,
Where the boughs rain when it blows.
Oh, never this whelming east wind swells
But it seems like the sea's return
To the ancient lands where it left the shells
Before the age of the fern;
And it seems like the time when after doubt
Our love came back amain.
Oh, come forth into the storm and rout
And be my love in the rain.
                    - *A Line-Storm Song*

Evan read again and closed his eyes, wishing to send this thought to Anna. He knew a literal and figurative storm loomed.

Anna glanced about the room, spotting dozens of gifts and keepsakes to complete. She could not focus. She needed to hear Evan's voice. Their relationship remained a perplexing paradox—a source of both great instability and great security.

She dialed his number. "Hi. It's just me."

"Hey, Anna! How are you?" Evan replied, no longer restraining his enthusiasm.

Anna felt a strange sense of relief—his fervor confirmation that she was not the only one consumed.

"I'm fine. What are you up to today?"

For sixty minutes, Anna didn't have a care in the world. She was caught up in conversation, her mouth fixed in a perpetual smile.

Bells jingling against the front door interrupted Anna's laughing. Time to go.

"When can I see you next, Anna?" Evan asked tenderly.

"I need some time, Evan."

"Okay," he replied.

She heard the excitement drain from his voice.

"It's just that I have to…" she began to explain.

"I know, Anna. I know."

His patient reassurance returned, intensifying Anna's longing to be with him.

"I'll call you, okay?"

Chapter 13

LAKE CHAMPLAIN sparkled. The sun glistened off fortresses of snow. In the aftermath of the blizzard, enormous plows cleared the streets, burying parking meters and road signs. Road crews packed dump trucks with mounds of snow destined for the lake's chilly waters. Evan trotted the downtown streets, a brisk wind forcing him to walk face down toward Anna's shop.

The long weekend brought no word from her. She had promised to call, but it had been nearly a week. Was she trying to make things work with David? He had picked up the phone countless times—even dialed her number—but then hung up. Her silence perplexed him, but he blamed it on the two feet of snow blanketing the area. It would have been difficult for Anna to call from home.

After years of separation, it amazed Evan how quickly he had grown dependent on her again. He could not shake the unnerving feeling when apart. He had decided to surprise her at the shop with a special snack. As he pulled the door open, he couldn't suppress his smile. He looked around, but did not see her. She must be working in the back. Good. A better surprise. He pictured Anna appearing, expecting a customer but instead seeing him. He could hear her ask sweetly, "What are you doing here?"

Anna appeared.

"What are you doing here?" she snapped.

Evan's mouth fell. Confidence drained from his face. "Well," he mumbled, "I just thought…"

"You should have thought before coming!" she scolded. "What if David or someone else saw you? I *am* married, Evan."

His mind reeled. Her head resting on his shoulder, her hands clutching his arm, her tender eyes. Only a few days ago. Now abruptly turning on him. Cold. Accusatory. "Anna, I don't understand. You haven't called for almost a week and I needed to see you. I miss…"

"That doesn't give you the right to show up here. I told you I would call when I was ready."

"I couldn't wait any…"

"That wasn't your choice to make, Evan."

"Anna, what's going on? Why are you acting like this?"

"What do you mean, me? I don't know. Why did you tell me to move on? You say you can't wait to see me so you come barging in, but you sure took your time coming back from South America."

Furious at her accusations, Evan started to ask her why she hadn't waited for him. But the better part of wisdom prevailed and Evan held his tongue. He stormed from the shop, the bell clanging violently against the door. He threw the snack into the nearest trashcan and stomped to his truck. Speeding home, he banged the steering wheel and cursed drivers whose only sin was sharing the same road.

Evan pulled into the driveway and looked up at his house. He dreaded its cold indifference, waiting for a phone call that may never come. It would be torture. Another night alone.

While Anna went home to be with David. They would eat dinner together, no doubt snuggling on the sofa watching television and laughing. And he would hold her at night as they drifted off to sleep. She would be warm in their bed and when she woke in the middle of the night, he would be there.

Evan slammed the truck into reverse and floored the accelerator, barreling out of his driveway. Tires squealed as he raced toward Route 7. He was going to find Anna's house. He had to see where she lived, where she spent time with that other man. All these years, he had resolved she was happy without him. He had seen her kiss her husband. His jealousy never raged. But now it was too close. He had felt her touch, seen the look in her eyes. She wanted to be with him.

Should he do something he had refused to do for the past four years—disrupt their marriage?

I lost her once. I cannot lose her again.

Especially not to *this* guy.

Evan and Anna belonged together. If she couldn't make the decision, maybe he should help her make it.

Evan raced to Burlington, finding a hotel with an updated phone book. He flipped the flimsy white pages. Collins. David and Anna Collins. He hated that name. She was Anna Matthews. Or Anna Forrester. He scowled as he scribbled their address and home phone number. Colchester. North of the city. Evan ran to his truck, then darted to the convenience store to pick up a detailed street map. He sat in the parking lot and unfolded the unwieldy map, searching the tiny street names. There it is. He stared at the map for a minute before tossing it to the floor. He was going to find their house and, well, that's all he knew. Aware that his jealousy now controlled him, Evan seemed unwilling to temper it. What did he have to lose?

He weaved through the subdivision, reading street signs and scanning the houses. He turned right on Adams and left onto Edgefield. Anna's street. His heart beat faster. Odd numbered houses on the left, even on the right. He peeked one more time at the scribbled address. 1265. That's it. He peered out the window, inching past. The clock read 5:35. He feared arousing suspicion from neighbors if he stopped in front. He continued through the subdivision and turned around at the next intersection. He pulled to a stop by the curb and exhaled. Okay, I've seen the house. I know where she lives. Now what?

Knowledge is not always good, he thought. He pictured Anna and David in the house together. The scenes of their life together gnawed at his stomach. Everything Evan dreamed of doing with Anna, she was doing with David. The little things were most disturbing. Cooking dinner and eating together, discussing the days' events, washing dishes, watching television, holding each other. Not to mention more intimate moments in the bedroom. He tried to guard his mind from this thought, but it was too late.

Why am I torturing myself? His stomach churned, his head throbbed. He had no answers, only questions.

A vehicle turned onto Edgefield and approached. It was Anna. Evan strained to see her face. God, she is beautiful. Why can't I be with her? He knew she would be furious and unforgiving for this appearance. Especially in front of neighbors. And possibly her husband.

She disappeared into the garage.

The sight of her softened him.

His resentment yielded to a more understanding perspective. He attributed her reaction today to tension and confusion. She faced the most difficult decision of her life. Nevertheless, her words stung and left him uneasy.

◆◆◆

Steam from the running bath fogged the mirrors. Anna disrobed, soaking in the warm, humid air. The novel remained in a basket on the floor. Against her better judgment, she reached down.

Kelli plodded to the bedroom, despising the thought of crawling into bed alone. A note beneath the comforter instructed her to look under the bed. She found a small box with a card, a handful of Hershey Kisses, a blue tee shirt and a picture of what appeared to be a gigantic horse with floppy ears.

I will be gone for one night, but if it were only one minute it would be too long. I wanted to give you my heart, but you already own it. So you'll have to settle for this little care package:

Put these kisses in your mouth so I can feel the warmth of your lips.

Wear my shirt close to your skin so I can touch you while you sleep.

Rest your sweet head on my pillow so I can gaze at you and feel the warm comfort of your breath all night.

Now click off the light and close your eyes. And know that I am thinking about you.

I MOOSE you.
Justin

Anna wanted to stay upset at Evan. She thought it would make her decision easier. But her anger dissolved in the consuming warmth of his love letters.

Evan could not stop the disturbing images. Anna and David in their house together. He sat brooding, staring out into hollow darkness. Facing the probability of resuming his life without her.

He stoked the fire a final time and returned to his chair, propping his feet on the ottoman. The wood crackled and spit sparks as he settled into Robert Frost.

All out of doors looked darkly in at him
Through the thin frost, almost in separate stars,
That gathers on the pane in empty rooms.
What kept his eyes from giving back the gaze
Was the lamp tilted near them in his hand.
What kept him from remembering what it was
That brought him to that creaking room was age.
He stood with barrels round him—at a loss.
And having scared the cellar under him
In clomping there, he scared it once again
In clomping off—and scared the outer night,
Which has its sounds, familiar, like the roar
Of trees and crack of branches, common things,
But nothing so like beating on a box.
A light he was to no one but himself
Where now he sat, concerned with he knew what,
A quiet light, and then not even that.
He consigned to the moon, such as she was,
So late-arising, to the broken moon
As better than the sun in any case

For such a charge, his snow upon the roof,
His icicles along the wall to keep;
And slept. The log that shifted with a jolt
Once in the stove, disturbed him and he shifted,
And eased his heavy breathing, but still slept.
One aged man—one man—can't keep a house,
A farm, a countryside, or if he can,
It's thus he does it of a winter night.

- An Old Man's Winter Night

The crisp morning air had cleared Evan's head. The phone was ringing as he returned from his morning walk. Paper and groceries fell to the floor.

"Hello?"

"Hi, Evan. It's me. I'm so sorry. I shouldn't have…"

"No, I shouldn't have come up. You were right."

"Evan, those things I said. I didn't mean them, really. I shouldn't have yelled at you."

Evan paused. "Anna, what's wrong?"

"I'm scared, Evan. I don't know what to do," she managed through sniffles.

"Is it about David?"

"That, and you and me."

"Can we talk about it?"

"Yes, but not on the phone."

"Why don't we meet at the Milton Inn for lunch? I can be there by eleven o'clock."

"That would be great."

"I'm sorry, Anna. I…"

"I am, too. Are you okay?"

"Yeah, but I still miss you."

"I miss you, too, Evan."

It marked the first time Anna had expressed her feelings with words. She had sidled up next to him and rested her head on his shoulder in the truck. But he knew saying those words was difficult, and therefore significant.

I miss you, too, Evan.

The sweet refrain played in his heart all morning.

Evan and Anna greeted each other with relieved smiles and tentative eyes. Walking quietly into the restaurant, Evan requested the same table they had previously. Food held no appeal. Anna was poised to tell the man she loved—about her husband. She worried that exposing her struggles would give Evan false hope, and she couldn't make any promises.

But Anna felt compelled to be honest with Evan. He remained her best friend and she trusted him completely. Still, her decision affected three lives, three futures.

"Anna, you don't have to tell me anything you don't want…"

"I know, but I need to tell you. I'm not sure where to begin, though. I met David a year after your last letter. I wasn't really excited about our relationship, but in time he became the comfort and stability I needed. He was a thoroughly decent man. And for some women, that's enough." Anna sighed. "He's what I *thought* I needed then, but he was not what I wanted. I wish…I wish I had made a different decision."

Evan studied her. "Are you in love with him?"

"I *love* him."

"But are you *in* love with him?"

"Do I get excited to see him or spend time with him? Do I look forward to the future with him? No. I care for him. But, no, I am not in love with him."

Anna struggled to explain. "David and I gaze at the sun setting on snow-capped peaks. We are there together, mentioning how beautiful it is, but we experience it separately. My enjoyment stems from the surroundings, not from being with *him*. There are whole parts of life— discussions, experiences, dreams—that will be shut off because I can't share them with him. That scares me."

Anna continued, relieved to release emotions trapped for so long. "You and I stand silently, knowing what the other is thinking, sharing it completely. It's *you* that I am enjoying. I don't know if that makes sense or not."

"Yeah, I understand. But if he knew all this, I'm sure he'd try to change."

"He knows I like to laugh and live passionately. A person can't learn that. And I can't ask him to be someone he's not." Anna's replies underscored how thoroughly she had considered the issues, how firmly she trusted her convictions. "It would be easier to leave him if he treated me badly or we were both dissatisfied."

Leave him.

It was the first time that phrase had escaped her mouth—a thought that added a measure of gravity to the discussion.

"Anna, is your relationship just stale because you've been together for awhile? Wouldn't this happen to us?"

"I've thought about that. And it's not the newness or the drama. It's the connection, Evan. You and I had it. We still have it. It's not what we do or say, but who we are. David and I are moving down separate paths. He wants a companion. I need a soul mate. I am only complete with you."

Anna fidgeted in her seat and looked at him. He remained quiet and listened.

"I don't know, Evan. I don't want to hurt him. If I stay, I can live a comfortable life, but I would be living a lie—lying to David, lying to myself."

She leaned in closer to him. "Evan, when we were apart, I was left hollow. You've walked inside and filled that space again. I'm afraid to lose you."

Chapter 14

THE EXPLOSION of the ax against the log created a thunderous clap, then a crunching tear as the blade ruptured the wood. The split was complete, as drops of sweat ran across Evan's temples and down his face despite the chill of the morning. He could not explain the satisfaction of slowly raising the weighted end of the ax high above his head—and in a swift, violent motion swinging the blade completely through the log, watching the split pieces fall to either side. Setting another log on edge, Evan brought his ax to bear, this time the blade failing to make it all the way through, leaving the wood hanging by sinewy threads. He kicked the pieces apart with his boots and continued laboring with steady rhythm. He would split five logs in a row at a furious pace before taking a short reprieve to straighten his back, stretching while wiping sweat from his brow and surveying the fruits of his labor. Another five blows and he would drop the ax and stack the wood in criss-cross piles. This wood would not heat his home until the following fall after it had dried thoroughly. But the satisfaction of chopping was immediate.

He placed the firewood in uneven piles beside a small stream bordering his property. Evan heard the trickle of water running through the partially frozen stream, melting snow feeding the continual flow. Water passed through fragile tunnels of ice, surfacing and spilling over small creek stones before disappearing once again below the ice.

He absorbed the Vermont countryside. Sitting inside waiting for Anna's call promised only torment. Out here he could think clearly and put his life in perspective. He had strolled into town at daybreak for his paper before returning to read while having breakfast. Around nine, he put on a pair of jeans, a worn flannel shirt and his heavy work boots. He planned to kill off the morning wait completing outdoor chores before checking at lunchtime for Anna's call.

For the next hour, Evan cleared the overgrown brush from the creek side, dragging the remnants through the snow to the far side of his property. Noon approached. He had waited long enough. He hurried to the house, refusing to stop to remove his snow-covered boots, and continued through the kitchen straight to the den. The red light flashed. His excitement grew.

"Hi, Evan? Will you call me when you get in? I'm at the shop."

Her voice was sweet, expectant. Evan removed his jacket, folding it across a nearby chair. Taking a deep breath, he dialed the number. Finally, after four or five rings, she picked up.

"Hey, Anna!"

"Evan! Where have you been?"

"Just out chopping some wood. How are you today?"

"Good. I was wondering," she began coyly, "if you would like to come by tomorrow and have lunch with me."

"Geez, I have to look at my calendar, Anna. You know I'm a busy man. Let's see...tomorrow...hmmm. I just happen to have a couple hours open in the middle of the day."

"You know, if you're too busy, Evan, we can wait until next week."

"Nope, I think I can fit you in."

"Good. I can't wait."

"I can't either. How about if I bring lunch for us?"

Anna liked that. She knew he was already planning a surprise. But she had her own plan.

"No. All I want you to bring is you."

Her unguarded expressions of affection surprised him. Containing his enthusiasm proved futile.

An overcast sky and blustery wind, along with the threat of additional snow, prevailed over the city. Arriving early as usual, Evan parked three blocks from Anna's shop. Her affection proved intoxicating. He darted in and out of pedestrian traffic, his feet moving swiftly over the frozen sidewalk. He told himself to calm down. He pictured her face—smiling, eyes sparkling. Just past a bench where an old man sat bundled in coat and hat, Evan crossed the street to Anna's shop. Valentine's Day gifts adorned the showcase. He reached for the doorknob and glanced into the store.

His smile vanished. His stomach sank.

He looked again, intently.

David was inside. Giving Anna a hug.

She smiled.

Deep breath. He backed away and staggered down the street, not wanting to be seen, not wanting to see anymore. A cavernous pain burrowed into him. He fell against an old bench, doubled over as if punched in the stomach.

He couldn't erase the smile from his mind. To hear her say she couldn't leave David would be painful. To carry the mental picture of her smiling with *him*, for the rest of his life, was devastating. Every word she had spoken about her relationship with David competed with that smile for the truth. A smile said she was happy. Happy to be with *him*.

It tormented him as the kiss had. On that very street. Four years ago. Both times he had come to see his Anna only to discover she was not his Anna at all. But this time hurt more. When he returned from South America, he had not spoken to Anna in years. He had no expectations, only distant hope. This time was different.

All I want you to bring is you.

What happened last night? Evan was convinced she had decided to stay and leave their relationship in the past. David was her future. After all, she said she could live a good, comfortable life with him.

Evan shuffled through the front door and sank into the sofa, flipping channels, rising only for a drink or trip to the bathroom. He stared listlessly for hours, frustrated that nothing could distract him. He could not eat, did not want to eat. The phone rang, but he could not listen to her voice.

Anna slammed the phone. Where was he? If something had come up, he would have called. It didn't make sense. Earlier in the day, she feared an accident. She had called area hospitals. No Evan Forrester or Morgan Jackson.

She eventually concluded that Evan had arrived early. He must have seen her with David. Again.

She remained distracted all night.

◆ ◆ ◆

A light snow began falling after dusk. It flitted down in big white flakes, slowly spotting the black asphalt. Evan stood by the window, looking across his fields, the uniform innocence of snowfalls past trodden and pocked by uneven melting, its brilliance muted by the subtle stains of fallen leaves and limbs. Evan watched with quiet approval as one snowflake after another spread swiftly like a patched quilt, softening the rutted landscape and renewing its purity. He ran upstairs and turned on floodlights to illuminate his property. It was a welcome distraction.

Since Evan had been a little boy, snow enthralled him. Waking up in the still of the night, scampering to the bedroom window, lifting on tiptoes, feeling the cold window against his cheek and twisting his head just so to catch a glimpse of the falling snow in the porch lights. Scurrying to the other side of the house, praying that roads were no longer distinguishable from sidewalks. Hoping for a day of sledding, snowball fights and building snowmen instead of being taunted through classroom windows. Trudging home through knee-high white powder, exhausted and famished. Seeking refuge with hands frozen and toes numb and wrinkled. Greeted at the door by a concerned Mom, her hands warm against crimson cheeks. The sound of slippery jackets being unzipped and dropping to the floor. Hats, gloves, pants and socks shed to join in a ragged bundle. Pulling on dry sweatpants, an oversized sweatshirt and wool socks. Thawing in front of the fireplace, sipping hot chocolate hidden by tiny marshmallows. Dipping grilled cheese sandwiches into steaming tomato soup. Warm and replenished, ready to attack the day once more. Limitless possibilities, only a few hours of daylight remaining.

He could feel it like it was yesterday. He built a fire and found a college basketball game to complete the night.

During breaks, Evan stood hands-in-pockets and watched the snow fall progressively harder. Within hours, the previous day's footprints had been covered. The game ended and Evan blew out the candles. One more trip to admire the falling snow. But admiration would not suffice.

Donning a heavy coat and scarf, Evan sat on the steps and jammed his feet into winter boots, lacing them hurriedly. The familiar gray sky appeared backlit by a moon that illuminated high, white clouds. Snow fell from every direction.

Evan trudged down the driveway and followed his morning path. Only now he ambled through town in the middle of the street, delighting in his freedom. He lost himself in the serenity of the moment, when it seemed only he and God were awake to prize the redemptive beauty. Snowflakes fluttered in the dim yellow glow of old, black lampposts. Untouched waves of snow drifted freely with every gust, surrounding him in a sea of white. In perfect tranquility, the only sounds snow crunching beneath his feet and the whispering wind. He tried to make sense of the situation with Anna, contemplating decisions that had shaped his life.

A delicate snowflake landed on his cheek with a wet splash. Evan let it melt into a pool of tiny droplets on his skin. The tracks he had made only minutes before were already softened by freshly fallen snow. Powder like angel's dust swirled off his rooftop and tickled his face. He knocked his boots against the steps and shook the snow from his coat, frozen crystals falling against his neck and down his shirt, causing an involuntary shiver. He changed into dry clothes and fell asleep, renewed and hopeful.

◆◆◆

Evan woke the next morning and succumbed to the flashing red light he had ignored.

"Evan, please call me. Are you okay? Call as soon as you get this."

"Hi, Evan. It's me. Are you there? Please pick up."

"Evan? It's Anna. Call me. I'll be here a few more minutes."

Three times he had made the trip to Burlington to see her. Three times he had left distraught.

Evan sat in his chair, looking out at the snow, the footprints from his midnight stroll hidden. He picked up the phone and called Anna, his stomach still uneasy.

"Good morning. This is Anna."

"Hi. It's Evan."

She heard his voice sapped of energy, knowing then what had happened.

"Evan, you saw David in the shop with me, didn't you?"

"You looked pretty happy in there, Anna. I guess things are okay with you two now. I should be happy for..."

"Evan, don't be ridiculous. That's not it at all and you should know better. I wasn't expecting him, but he was downtown for a meeting and decided to stop by. I knew you were going to be there in a little while. I tried to move him along as..."

"I guess I got there a little too early and saw a little too much."

"What do you mean, Evan? Do you know what we were talking about?" It sounded harsh, but she had to counter his sulking.

"No, but I saw you hug him. And then I saw you with a big smile."

"Evan, think about it. If he hugs me, I can't turn and run. And do you know why I was smiling? He told me his sister was pregnant." She let out an exasperated gasp. "Evan, it's hard to explain, but I only smile *with* him. With you, it's different. Remember what I told you the other day? I smile at you, because of you. You don't have to say anything. You make me smile because when I am with you, I am happy."

"Oh, I guess I..."

"Wasted an entire day moping around wondering whether I wanted to be with you?"

Even in the face of an obvious jab, he couldn't resist smiling. "Something like that."

"Well, you stood me up, Mister. And I expect repayment."

"Could I suggest we meet someplace other than your shop, Anna?" They both laughed. "I know we won't be able to celebrate Valentine's Day together on the fourteenth, but would you go to the Gorge with me later this week?"

"I would love to, Evan."

Chapter 15

HER LIGHT brown hair bounced playfully, long ringlets dangling past her ears, drawing Evan's eyes to her neckline. A red cashmere sweater and black jeans accentuated her figure in a way that made it difficult to concentrate. A black wool coat lie folded across her arms. She climbed into the truck and greeted Evan with a warm smile. She was stunning.

The bright sun concentrated its force in the truck. The outside temperature pushed fifty degrees, unseasonably warm for a February afternoon. Still, the air would be brisk at Cynthiana Gorge. Though Valentine's Day remained a week away, this would be their only opportunity to celebrate together—enjoying a picnic at the canyon.

Blissful. Content. One afternoon in which to capture this elation—every word, every laugh, every touch, every gaze— and lock it up in their hearts and minds. If they tried hard enough, they could make a minute last longer than sixty seconds, they thought.

They settled in for the short ride over familiar terrain. Snow mottled shaded hillsides and the evergreens grew dense as they climbed toward the overlook. The constant conversation and laughter mixed with vivid memories of the

Gorge. But it wasn't the natural beauty or any particular activity that made it special. There were no distractions—just the two of them.

The truck rocked side to side as the tires edged off smooth pavement into the small dirt lot, a cloud of dust rising slowly behind them. Evan glanced at Anna.

"Thanks for doing this, today."

"Stop thanking me," she replied softly. "I wouldn't want to be anywhere else."

"It's going to be chilly out there, you know."

"Well, maybe I can find a big, strong man somewhere to keep me warm," Anna said with reassuring smile. She knew he frustrated easily, wanting to make the experience perfect. He had expressed regret that it wasn't a warm spring day, when the sweet perfume of lilacs floated on gentle breezes and wildflowers bloomed along the trail.

They bounded from the truck. Evan heaved a large pack on his back, offering to share the space with Anna. She placed a gift inside and zipped it shut.

Evan reached out his hand. Anna folded her hand into his.

Tingles charged up her forearm, electricity and warmth spreading through her body. Her knees felt faint, steps unsteady. She staggered forward, inattentive to everything around her.

They stopped abruptly. Anna stumbled into Evan's arm, shaking her from her daze. Their trail was overgrown. Branches and bushes protruded over the path blotched with encroaching groundcover. He glanced over to the established trails, then plodded forward, holding back limbs for Anna, sliding sideways, squeezing through tight spaces. Anna watched him struggle, focused and determined, refusing to follow the paths everyone else chose. Robert Frost—he who took the road less traveled—inspired Anna as a young woman. It was one of the reasons she had fallen in love with Evan.

Only he wanted to take the road that *no one* had traveled.

He apologized repeatedly, but Anna assured him she was fine. Evan found his footing and although it remained unfamiliar to her, he was confident they were on their path. Squirrels played games of tag, rustling leaves and scurrying up trees, winding in circles before scampering back through the leaves again. The woods provided protection from the wind while the vigorous hike warmed them. Their hands never parted. The roar of the whitewater grew louder. Reaching the clearing where the huge rock jetted out over the canyon, shrill gusts cut through them. Evan pulled Anna around to the south side of the rock, finding a sheltered crevice.

He held her hand as she stooped to sit on the rock. Immediately, she sprang to her feet. Evan laughed. Anna slapped his arm and playfully punched at him.

"You knew it was frozen, didn't you?"

Evan tried to reply, but was giggling too hard. "Well, it's not like we're in Miami. It *is* Vermont in February," he finally muttered.

He lowered his pack and pulled out two wool blankets. He spread one beneath them and beckoned for Anna to sit with him in warmth. He had left enough slack to cover their legs. Once settled, he draped the other blanket around their shoulders. They surveyed the Gorge, taking turns pointing out scenic views throughout the ravine.

"Hey, look," Evan motioned.

"Where?"

Evan inched closer to Anna, his leg now resting against hers. Even through jeans, they immediately felt the warmth and magic of their touch. Evan leaned in and pressed his cheek against hers, trying to line up her sight of vision. He signaled with his outstretched left arm to a spot beyond his pointing index finger.

"See them?" he asked softly.

She felt his slightly rough stubble brushing against her soft skin, warm on her face. She closed her eyes for a few seconds. Time, stand still. But he was talking and wanting her to look. And the more he talked, the more lost she became. She was taking in a familiar scent that still intoxicated her, aroused her. A mix of his skin, his cologne and even his breath—that took her back to a time she wished she had never left. In the midst of the cold, she felt flush, warm. She struggled to concentrate, not wanting to find the scene below.

Evan fought the urge to turn and look into her. There would be no going back. Her nose would be cold against his skin, her tongue melting into his, dizzying, fingers tracing face and neck and hair, bodies pressing, gazing, passion kindled more frantically still. They would stop for a moment, breathless, overcome with desire, love, yearning. He would slowly draw her mouth into his, their tongues full, warm and complete, absorbing each other deeply.

They held their breath and remained still. Their lips were inches apart, longing to touch.

"See? Right there?" Evan broke the silence.

"Uh huh," Anna mumbled weakly.

A doe and two fawns crossed a meandering stream. The deer played amid snowy banks and crystal water bubbling over the stony creek bottom. Evan and Anna watched the deer until they disappeared into the thick underbrush.

Evan surveyed the grandness of the Gorge. Anna knew the look in his eyes. He was somewhere else. She wrapped her arm inside his and whispered into his ear. "What are you thinking about?"

He paused, then whispered back.

"You."

The way he said it. Simply. Forcefully. Airily. Tingles shattered her composure. She could still feel the warm impress of his lips touching her ear. She sat still, wanting him.

"Will you tell me what you are picturing?"

"Do you really want to know?"

"Of course."

Evan began describing Christmas together, hesitantly at first, then gaining momentum. But there was a new dimension to his stories. Again.

He and Anna were not the sole focus of the dreams. There were children. *Their* children. *Their* family. At first, Anna thought he had taken his cue from the family of deer below. But it was more than that. The quality of detail in his accounts made it clear he had been thinking about their family life. He wasn't reliving the past, he was planning the future.

He described scenes of family life that made her heart flutter. He knew her, how fondly she recalled her childhood, the importance of family. She could see candles in windows, gingerbread men and candy canes dangling from the fresh Christmas tree, their children leaving Santa a note with cookies and milk.

Anna joined in and added to the scene. She strung sentence after sentence together, hands and eyes expressive. They inspired each other and took turns painting the picture until it became their story, the portrait of their life together.

They did not want to leave that place. They could feel it, taste it, smell it.

They soaked in the experience, pondering their relationship, willing time to slow. Meeting in the bookstore had changed their lives nearly a decade ago. An unexpected encounter at the same college had changed them again. The emotions felt foreign, yet natural. The picture of their future had not faded, but become clearer—the lines more defined, the backdrop more complete, the colors more brilliant. And its reality closer than ever.

The hours slipped away. Evan broke the silence. "So are you ready for the gourmet lunch I prepared?"

"Strawberry or grape?" Anna replied dryly, her brows turned down in mock disgust.

"Strawberry, of course."

Evan happily unveiled a brown paper bag and placed their meal before them. "The special today, ma'am, is freshly baked whole wheat bread, spread with a succulent blend of ground, roasted peanuts and garden fresh strawberries, handpicked and preserved only eighteen months ago in a jam sauce that is to die for. Really, it is," Evan said with a straight face. Anna's eyes absorbed him. This was the Evan she had fallen in love with. "Complementing the main course is potatoes au chip, made with care by a very religious sect in Pennsylvania Dutch country with spuds imported from Idaho. You will be pleased to know that we will be sipping on a fine white beverage with a hearty fizz that may tickle your nose and cause embarrassing burps. Drink with care. And if you are able to keep this meal down, you may look at our fabulous dessert table." Evan dramatically revealed his dessert. "Featuring...moist, delicious brownies. With walnuts, of course."

"Awwww. Little heart-shaped brownies. How did you remember I love walnuts?"

"Well, it only took me three tries to get these right. I hope you like them."

"How do you eat, you poor man?" She was joking, but genuinely wondered what a man so lacking in culinary skills ate to maintain his weight and health.

They sat contentedly, eating their sandwiches and enjoying the gorge. They talked about the shop, her family and the wonders around them. He explained how he had purchased enough eggs, mix and chopped walnuts to make three pans of brownies. The third batch turned out so well he was afraid to touch it. He finally carved the hearts out with a sharp knife. Hence the irregular shapes.

Anna couldn't resist laughing at him. But she loved him for it. He had turned an ordinary lunch into an unforgettable experience. Evan fed her the last potato chip.

"Do I get my brownies now?" she asked like a little girl.

"All your crumbs eaten?"

"Yep."

Evan gave Anna three brownies and watched as she bit into the first one. "Mmmm. Evan, this is actually really good. I'm proud of you!"

"You're not just saying that?" he asked with uncertainty. Here was this man sitting beside her—accomplished, confident, successful. He was a man to her in every sense, yet at times he exuded a boyish innocence she found endearing.

"Really," she reinforced, squeezing his leg. "I love them."

She savored two brownies and dropped the remaining one in the plastic bag. "I want to save this one."

"Anna, I have something for you for Valentine's Day. I hope you aren't disappointed with…"

"Evan, if all we did was sit out here and eat a sandwich together, that would be more than enough. I am so happy."

139

"It really isn't much. There are many things I want to give you and I had lots of ideas, but I knew you wouldn't be able to…"

"I know, Evan. Don't worry."

Evan reached into his pack and pulled out a gift bag. "So I didn't have to wrap it, of course," he said.

"Probably saved a tree," she jibed.

Anna peered into the bag and gently pulled the white tissue aside, revealing a poem titled, "Valentine Dreams" handwritten in black ink on parchment paper.

"I wanted to write something that no one else gets to read, just you."

Anna smiled and read.

> I dream of waking in the night to watch you sleep
> Listening to your every breath
> Amazed by your innocence
>
> I dream of waking up next to you
> Your voice the first song in my ear
> Your lips the first taste of the day
>
> I dream of tears of sadness and tears of joy
> Falling on my shoulder, stinging my skin
> But always intermingled with my own
>
> I dream of lifting your veil with quivering hands
> And beholding beauty and life
> My bride
>
> I dream of kneeling in silence before God
> Pleading for help to be a better man
> Giving thanks for the angel beside me

I dream of good times and hard times
Savoring each laugh
Growing closer in adversity

I dream of watching you when you are unaware
Toiling in your garden, creating with your hands
You

I dream of white satin dresses, little curls
Dolls and mud pies and squeals
A little girl in her daddy's arms

I dream of tussled hair and tussled clothes
Dirty face and bandaged fingers
A little boy in his mommy's arms

I dream of holding hands on a hot summer day
Swearing we won't let go no matter how hot it gets
And keeping our promise

I dream of gazing at you from afar
Overwhelmed by your beauty
Moved by your grace

I dream of snuggling at night warm and secure
You falling asleep to the pulse of my heart,
Hearing every beat whisper your name.

I dream of rocking on our porch together
Into the sunset of our lives
Looking over at you and seeing my best friend

I dream of the day when I no longer have to dream
Only be
With my dream come true

You complete me, Anna. I need you.

Yours forever,
Evan

Tears cascaded. She fell into his arms, buried her head in his chest, and clutched him tightly. She listened to his heart, afraid to let go. Evan slipped her a wrinkled napkin. Dabbing her eyes, Anna looked deeply into his.

"Do you know I hate you? Why do you have to be so sweet?"

Evan held her close, kissing her head and slowly stroking her hair. A few minutes later, she reached around him and grabbed the pack. Still sniffling, she told him to close his eyes. The faint calls of birds echoed through the canyon, their cries muffled by trees rustling in a brisk wind.

Anna placed a small, exquisitely wrapped gift in his lap. Evan traced the edges of the rectangular package between his thumb and index finger, then flipped it over and peeled the taped edges of wrap. He could feel Anna's gaze. He cupped the paper in his hand and pulled it away from the gift, revealing the back of a frame. A picture, he thought, of he and Anna together. Or perhaps a drawing.

He placed it face up. Evan and his father stood side by side, smiling widely, his dad's arm around him. He pored over the picture, absorbing the details. Slow, quiet tears climbed over his eyelids and dripped down his cheeks.

"Where did you find this, Anna?" Evan asked, revering the photograph.

"I wasn't sure if it was appropriate for Valentine's Day or…"

"It's perfect, Anna." Evan brushed the corners of his eyes with his sleeve. "Perfect."

Anna put her arm through his and rested her head. She studied his face as he stared at the picture. Her strong man. Her little boy. Tough and adventurous one moment. Tender and settled the next.

"Where did you get this?"

"I have a hope chest where I keep all your letters and photographs of us. Remember your family reunion the summer after we met? I took this photograph of you and your dad." Anna spoke softly. "You used to tell me you two didn't get along, but I could see it in his eyes. He was proud of you *then*, Evan."

His chin quivered. He choked back tears and held the picture tightly with both hands. His father embraced him. Evan had not remembered it that way.

"Anna, thank you. You don't know how much this means to me."

And yet he knew she did. She took time to search for this photo. She doubtless had seen dozens, if not hundreds of photographs of she and Evan together. Most people would have chosen a picture to be remembered by. But Anna chose to frame a photograph of Evan and his dad. It spoke volumes about her. How well she knew him. How much she loved him.

The sun disappeared behind thick clouds. The wind shifted, slicing through them like a razor. But they sat there still, huddling closer together. Clutching their gifts, staring at them occasionally through eyes watered from strong gusts. Anna leaned in and rested on Evan's shoulder, closing her eyes and squeezing his hand. It didn't matter that it was cold, that they ate peanut butter and jelly sandwiches, that the rock was uncomfortable, that they couldn't be sitting alone by a warm fire. It didn't matter that they couldn't exchange romantic gifts or have an entire Valentine's Day and night together.

Blissful.

Anna sat straight back in the truck, refusing to gather her things while Evan made his way around to her door. He caught her mournful eyes and reluctantly opened the door.

"Yeah, I know. I don't want you to go, either."

She wanted to leave with him and never come back. Begin a new life. "Thank you for today, Evan. It was perfect."

"You make it that way, Anna."

"I'm not going to see you next week, am I?"

"No, but I'll call you if that's okay."

Anna drove slowly, the poem cradled in her lap. At every stoplight, she read another stanza. He had not mentioned love one time. He didn't have to. It was better left unsaid. He didn't talk about homes or vacations or cars or things they would do together. It was simply about being. Small things they would share, he would appreciate. She counted the dreams. Fourteen. Must be for February fourteenth, she thought. It was so Evan.

She read the words. *My bride.* Not *my wife. My bride.* More intimate. Praying for strength to be a better man. Children. A boy and a girl, as she had always pictured it.

You complete me. I need you.

He's not trying to convince me how good he would be for me, she noticed. He's telling me what I mean to him. How very different.

Once again, he was roaming inside, opening the door to that deep place.

Susan had asked if Anna had fallen in love with the carefree days of her youth. Today's events convinced Anna she loved Evan more now than ever. The same qualities that attracted her ten years ago remained. But, years had added depth to him, a depth she found overwhelming.

Chapter 16

EVAN ARRIVED in Boston at eleven-thirty to eat lunch with the manager of a large bookstore. Evan had arranged a series of signings throughout the area to support a Valentine's Day promotion. He knew readers appreciated the opportunity to meet him, and he genuinely enjoyed the personal connection with his fans.

He often felt uneasy at the thought of strangers peering through a private window into his soul. The books weren't about fictional characters. They were about Evan. And Anna. But he took comfort in understanding that only he and Anna knew.

He was thankful for the opportunity to travel and work during this holiday. It would keep his mind occupied. Being at home so close to Anna, but still apart, would be unbearable.

After lunch, Evan entered the store and recognized the familiar scene. People walked through the doors, excited to meet him, welcoming the respite from the February chill. Soon they began shifting their weight, trying to balance their discomfort and minimize their weariness. Jackets peeled off. The store, which seemed properly heated with twenty people browsing, became oppressive once hundreds of fans pressed in. Evan grew irritated at store managers whose lack of foresight drove customers away and made those who stayed miserable.

He often requested that host stores provide snacks and drinks, and asked if women with toddlers tugging at their legs could move forward. He did everything he could to make the experience pleasant.

Evan looked up at the long line and smiled. He greeted fan after fan, engaging in small talk and graciously thanking each person.

In the midst of the crowd, Evan felt lonelier than ever.

An abundance of hearts and all things red signaled the approaching Valentine's Day. The next three days would be chaotic until closing. Unlike many holidays for which people shopped early, the purchase cycle for Valentine's Day was compressed into final hours and minutes. Men, in particular, frequented the shop on the fourteenth, walking from downtown offices, hoping Anna would have the perfect gift. And she usually did. Otherwise, they were left to rummage through picked-over remnants on drug store shelves. She stocked a large variety of baskets featuring floral arrangements and stuffed animals along with a special assortment of cards. Anna welcomed the busyness. It kept her occupied and provided the first boost to sales since Christmas.

She tried to use the time apart from Evan wisely. Although she wanted to give up, she felt obligated—to David, herself and even Evan—to explore all possibilities with her husband. She hated the word obligated, but that's how she felt. If she intended to leave, the decision had to be firm, without reservation.

Anna replayed good memories with David that shaped their relationship. Their courtship, his proposal, the wedding, their first home, opening her shop.

She pleaded for the feelings to come back. She felt only a strange ambivalence.

And now frustrated. She couldn't pinpoint the bad times. There weren't any.

Anna determined to light a spark between them. She ignored the voice inside repeating the inevitable, that there was nothing to kindle. She had to give David a chance—he deserved that much.

Evan tossed in bed, examining the hotel room. It was cold and impersonal. How many people had stayed here before? Evan wondered about their stories. Thousands of people had lived in this room for at least a night, but day in and day out it looked exactly the same. Same soap. Same bedspread. Same curtains. Towels rolled taut on the vanity the same way every day.

He had made it through three successful days of book signings. He was scheduled to work the following day from noon until three and then return to Middlebury. Though he missed home, he dreaded the loneliness while Anna celebrated with David. He clicked off the bedside lamp and slumped under the sheets, telling himself they would be together soon.

Anna hunted for clues. She sat in the living room, searching photo albums filled with snapshots. She needed to find a gift, something special and unexpected. Something that he could get excited about. David was in the den working. Poor man,

148

she thought. He works so hard. And God knows it isn't exciting work. She rose to pour a mug of hot cocoa and asked David if he would like some, too. Orange juice, please. Anna took him a glass of juice, asking how his work was progressing and patting his back. She wished she had the desire to kiss him. But it wasn't there. Not yet, anyway. He thanked her without looking up from his work.

Anna returned to the sofa, noticing Evan's latest book nearby. Unable to resist, she searched for a favorite excerpt.

"What did you get me for Valentine's Day, honey?" Kelli pried.

"Who says I got you anything? You know I love you, honey. Let's just have a quiet night, okay?"

For Christmas, Justin and Kelli had taken an extended vacation to Europe, spending the holidays in small Bavarian towns nestled among the Swiss Alps. They celebrated Christmas with a German family, immersing themselves in centuries-old traditions. They had agreed to enjoy a simple night together.

"How is work today?"

"Fine, I'm preparing for a meeting with Bob from twelve to two. Are you going to work out?"

"Just about to leave. Have a good day, honey. And don't work too hard. You're going to need lots of energy tonight."

Plan one worked, he thought. Expectations lowered.

Kelli shouldn't have been surprised. But she was. In the car, her favorite flowers. Daisies. She opened the envelope. On the cover of the card, two tiny bears stood hand-in-hand.

I cannot *bear* to be apart from you any longer.

149

Meet me at Rembrandt's for lunch. One o'clock.
I will be the one gazing at you with wonder.
Captivated and distracted,
Justin
Kelli felt foolish standing by her car grinning so
widely. She hurried home to call Justin. "I thought you
had a meeting with Bob today?"
"I did, but I rescheduled. The thought of spending
Valentine's Day at lunchtime with him made me feel
like, you know…vomiting."
Kelli laughed out loud.
"Besides, I kinda miss someone already today."
"Kinda? And who would that be, Mr. Williams?"
Justin lowered his voice. "Well, it's this really
amazing girl. I'm madly in love with her. But don't tell
her. I sort of wanted to surprise her. Anyway, I was
hoping I could meet her for lunch today."
"For that, you can have her for breakfast, lunch and
dinner!"
"I'm actually in the mood for dessert. But, first
things first. One o'clock okay?"
"I can't wait."

A quaint sandwich and dessert shop in the art
district, Rembrandt's boasted a courtyard reminiscent
of a Mediterranean café. Sparkling eyes and a lingering
kiss greeted Justin, his reward complete. They enjoyed
conversation and laughs over a leisurely lunch, sharing
a slice of chocolate pie afterward. Kelli noticed he had
not glanced at his watch once. Justin suggested she
browse the galleries and enjoy the sunshine. He had to
return to the office.

"So when will I see my Valentine tonight?"

"I'm planning to sneak out a little early. How about that?"

"I'll be waiting for you."

It was the kind of night they loved—the anticipation building all day. Justin left the office a little after four. Someone had been lurking near his truck. He opened an envelope left on his seat. Inside was a grainy black and white card with schoolboy innocently kissing a little girl. "I am so glad you're mine," Kelli had written.

He sprang through the front door, greeted with hugs from his two favorite girls—Kelli delivering a tender kiss while their four-year-old clung to his leg. The evening went as planned.

After tucking Jessica in bed, they softened the lights and enjoyed a glass of wine while fixing dinner. Justin wrapped his arms around Kelli, playfully whispering in her ear as she tried to mix a salad. When the pasta was almost ready, he excused himself to build a fire in the living room. While the kindling began to catch, Justin unwrapped two wrought iron candleholders that accented the cozy room. They ate together by flickering light, music in the background, the fire crackling.

Plates and half-empty glasses were left scattered across the floor. They wanted each other, their lips and hands grasping up the winding stairs to the bedroom. Justin lay Kelli down and hovered above her, admiring and quietly tracing the contours of her face, her cheekbones, her eyes and nose and mouth, brushing

151

soft strands of hair behind her ears, eyes never leaving hers, shared passion reflected in his own. He cradled her in the safety of his arms, her head nestled in his strength as he pressed deeply into her. Kelli relinquished herself to him, her arms above her head revealing a body wanting to be touched and taken. The warm desire of his mouth melted into her neck, her body pulsing in waves. He felt the rhythms of her body respond to his touch. He met her eyes again. Their tongues were warm, swollen with need, craving more. She arched her back and gave herself to him completely, and he devoured her.

Kelli closed her eyes and drew him deeper. She felt the heat of his chest on her skin, his weight pressing into her, filled, complete. His hands clasped hers, arms outstretched. They held tight, the tension heightening the sensations, arms trembling, legs weak.

She felt something slide onto her finger.

He caught her gaze as she admired the emerald birthstone ring she had asked for many months before. The questions and words of appreciation could wait.

He took her to another place where only the two of them existed, where she no longer noticed the walls or ceiling. She became one with her lover, her best friend and the moment itself.

Chapter 17

STEAM LIFTED off the water, hovering above the Charles River at daybreak. Soft morning light illuminated the Boston skyline, reflecting gently off towering glass skyscrapers. Yellow cabs passed in unending succession. Evan followed the running path along the bank of the Charles, a crew team vigorously rowing in the opposite direction. He turned through a park dotted with proud statues of revolutionary heroes. Three city blocks to go, passing a crowded Starbucks and numerous bagel shops. He sprinted the final two minutes through the Commons, then crossed the street to his hotel, dodging screaming cars and jubilantly hopping the curb. He rode the elevator to the ninth floor, catching his breath and collapsing on the bed in his room. He would shower, order room service and await Anna's call.

Anna shivered and adjusted the heat. The hard overnight freeze had penetrated the cement walls and lingered. She drew the cocoa's warmth through her hands and mouth. Though she had spoken to Evan briefly each morning this week, she considered skipping the call today. She wanted to devote herself entirely to David on Valentine's Day. But not hearing Evan's voice would leave her unsettled. Knowing Evan would be upset would keep her distracted as well.

Their conversation was brief, their sentiments unspoken.
As she placed the phone on the counter, it rang.

"Happy Valentine's Day, honey!" David exclaimed.

"Hi, honey. Happy Valentine's Day," Anna replied.

"What are you doing?"

"Just getting ready to open the shop." Same time, same
questions, only today was Valentine's Day. Deep breath. Be
patient, be sweet.

"Listen, honey, I know I have been really busy lately
and…"

"It's okay, David. I know you have to work like…"

"No, Anna. Really, I'm going to make it up to you
tonight. It's going to be perfect."

"Well, I have something special for you, too."

"Okay. Have a good day."

Anna sighed. That wasn't so bad, she thought. He was
excited about his plans.

I'm going to make it up to you today.

But what did he mean? Spending more time together was
not the solution. He could not do anything to *make it up.* And
what was he thinking, that *one day* of surprises could
somehow change everything?

With the lunchtime crowd thinning, a young man strode
through the front door and handed Anna an exquisite vase
overflowing with a dozen red roses. Milling customers
acknowledged her self-conscious look with smiles and nods.
Anna opened the small card attached.

Your favorite flowers for my favorite girl.

Happy Valentine's Day, Anna!

Love,

David

It was sweet. They were beautiful. And Anna hated herself for not being excited or happy about them. She was trying—God she was trying—to appreciate her husband. But he was oblivious. Roses were not her favorite flower. Daisies were. Evan had remembered. It's insignificant, she told herself. David's intentions were good. Yet how many other women were receiving the same gift today?

She stared at the roses, but felt only disappointment they weren't daisies from Evan. Anything from Evan. She tried to suppress thoughts of him. The pressure left her with a splitting headache.

Evan continued signing books until four-thirty-five. He had agreed to accommodate the unexpectedly large crowd. How could he turn away so many people? More men stood in line today, his book a decent gift for a sweetheart, Evan thought.

He began the four-hour drive toward Middlebury, preoccupied with a question posed by a middle-aged woman.

"What are you doing with your Valentine tonight?" the woman had asked. "She must be very special."

"Just a quiet night at home," he replied awkwardly.

The question troubled him all afternoon. One after another, he met hundreds of people giving his book to the ones they loved.

While he sat home without Anna. As he had for many years.

Anna locked the shop door and hurried to her car. She planned to surprise David before dinner to set the atmosphere. Though she could find a thousand gifts for Evan, looking for David left her uninspired. He always smiled and said, "This is really nice, honey." His response deflated her enthusiasm and made the experience less meaningful.

The prospect of telling David she intended to leave complicated her choice. A romantic gift would not be genuine. But she was excited about the gift she had finally chosen for David.

She greeted him at the door at six o'clock, folded his coat over a chair and set his briefcase on the floor. "I've got some surprises for you." David wanted to change clothes and go to dinner, but Anna led him upstairs, trying to stay focused. She handed him a wrapped box. "Happy Valentine's Day, honey!"

"Don't you want to wait until later to…" he began.

"No. I want to do yours now. Open it."

"Okay," he agreed, his preoccupation obvious.

He unwrapped the box. A pair of long underwear. A perplexed look.

"What are…"

"Come on, you'll see. Just go with it." She struggled to resist images of Evan ripping into the box, eyes lit, thoroughly engaged in the adventure. Anna led David down the hallway to the guest bedroom. "Keep your eyes closed!"

"Okay, open!" David glanced about the room, spotting a sleeping bag on the floor. More puzzled. "Go ahead. Lie down."

David reluctantly sat down, confused. "Camping? Are we going camping together? Is that my Valentine's surprise?"

"Come on, David. Lie down."

"I feel stupid here in my…"

"Just wait. Now close your eyes again. Remember what you dreamed of becoming when you were a boy?"

"I don't know, Anna."

"Open your eyes, David."

Stars and moons and galaxies came to life, glowing above him. A grin crossed his face.

"An astronomer."

"I thought it was time to experience your dream."

She handed him a large box from the closet. As he pried open the thick cardboard flaps, Anna tried to make sense of her feelings. She loved him and wanted him to be happy. But she realized her love was sentimental, friendly, perhaps familial.

But not the love a wife has for her husband.

"You've got warm clothes, a sleeping bag and a telescope. Now all you need is a clear sky, and I tried to arrange that, too!" She pulled the cord and lifted the blinds to reveal a clear February sky.

"Anna, thank you. This is really nice." He set the pieces on the floor and stood to kiss her. "How did you think of the telescope?"

"I noticed how interested you were in that science show last week, and I remembered what you had said about being a kid and looking up at the stars and..."

"Maybe after tax season is over, I can really get into this. You ready to go to dinner?"

"I guess. Don't you want to put it together and..."

"No, I'm hungry. I can do that another time. Let's go eat."

Anna and David retreated to their bedroom. David changed clothes and talked about his day at work. His words dispersed into empty air as she stared in the mirror. Her chin quivered while she fought for control. *Why do I want to be with Evan so badly? Why can't I love David the same way?*

As she leaned closer to brush on fresh powder, she imagined Evan's warm hands around her waist, the force of

Kirk Martin

his body pressing against hers, whispering sweet "thank you's" in her ear. He would be teasing her with scenes of sharing a blanket under the heavens, discovering the stars, wondering aloud, making love. Together. They would no doubt be *late* for dinner. The joy of giving would be made complete by his reaction, and they would share it fully.

"Do what, honey," she asked, startled out of her daydream. "What did you say?"

"What tie should I wear with this?"

She turned to look at David. "How about the burgundy one?"

Anna finished applying mascara and lipstick. Backing away from the mirror, one last look. I wish Evan were here. What would he say?

The drive to dinner was quiet. David glanced over at Anna. "Are you okay?"

"I'm fine." She was lost.

"Did you like your roses today?"

"Yes, they were beautiful, David. Customers commented on them all afternoon."

Anna gathered herself and engaged in conversation as they turned a familiar corner. Cappucitti's remained one of their favorite spots, usually reserved for special occasions. A formal, romantic restaurant known for authentic dishes from southern Italy.

A slender vase with single red rose graced each table as candlelight shadows danced around them. Hushed conversations played below weeping violins while flames cast warmth from a stone fireplace.

"I love it here," Anna said, trying to put thoughts of Evan away. She focused on David. This was *their* place.

The waiter poured the wine and placed the carafe on the table. David lifted his glass. "To my Valentine. I love you." David presented Anna with an envelope and small package.

After reading a romantic card, she picked up the gift expectantly. She removed the bow and ribbon, unpeeling red and gold paper. She lifted the top of the small box. A diamond necklace sparkled in the candlelight, reflecting in crystal glasses. "It's absolutely beautiful, David. Thank you."

"You're welcome," he replied. She slipped it around her neck. "Anna, it's gorgeous on you."

"Would you mind if I excuse myself to see it?"

Anna walked through the restaurant, fumbling for clarity. It was *the perfect* night. A nice surprise at home, a romantic dinner and a stunning necklace. Why can't I feel anything for him?

She again found herself before a mirror, looking with desperation into eyes that offered no answers.

Evan closed the book abruptly and stared into the dark night. His hands fidgeted as he sat in his den, loud music driving in the background. No fire tonight. No love songs. No writing. Nothing to remind him that it was Valentine's night. He read a book detailing the role Vermont played in helping runaway slaves gain their freedom via the Underground Railroad. Evan read voraciously to satisfy his curiosity and thirst for learning. The more he read, though, the more he found to explore. He knew it was endless. Although the book fascinated him, Evan could not concentrate. He stood to refill his drink and change the CD, wondering what Anna was doing.

◆ ◆ ◆

"How do you picture us in five years? I mean, what will our life be like?" Anna probed.

"Umm. I've never really thought about that. I guess I've been so busy with work that I…"

"Well, think about it now. In five years or maybe even in ten. What do you see?" Anna peered intently.

David paused for a moment. "Well, I guess, you know, I'll hopefully be promoted to Partner and maybe we'll be in a bigger house, in one of those really nice subdivisions we've looked at. I don't know, maybe have a couple kids by then."

"Do you have any pictures in your mind, or maybe words to describe what it will feel like?"

"We'll be happy, if that's what you mean," he shot back, a hint of frustration in his voice. "I'm not sure what you want to hear."

"Don't just tell me what you think *I* want to hear. I want to know what *you* think, how *you* picture it."

"I told you," he began defensively, "I haven't really thought about it. I just see life moving along and getting promoted and your shop doing well, and having kids and playing outside. You know, the whole American dream thing." He smiled, a little unsure, but wanting Anna to know they would have a good life.

The homemade pasta, mouth-watering only minutes before, lost its flavor.

Trees and leaves and entire woods lay silhouetted in black out Anna's window. She stared into countryside void of definition. David zipped over winding roads, searching the radio for appropriate music. She had hoped something would be sparked inside. But she couldn't force an intimate relationship. Neither would she be complete without it.

◆ ◆ ◆

Evan tossed and turned all night. Anna had spent the most romantic night of the year with another man. His impatience and insecurity gave way to a fleeting desperation. But, what was he thinking? He couldn't confront David. Anna would despise him. *She* needed to make the decision.
He needed to hear her voice, to know her reassurance. The words would not release him.
She must be very special.

Anna lie still in bed, swallowed by darkness, pondering David's responses. His job came first. She knew he didn't mean it like that, but everything he mentioned was outward, impersonal. *A couple kids.* Not *our children* or *a little boy and girl.* Just another thing that the typical suburban couple is supposed to have. Like a big house. His Valentine's card, while romantic, was printed with a stranger's words. He had simply signed his name. She didn't doubt his love for her.
But his love left her empty.

Chapter 18

"SUSAN, I can't do this anymore."

"Do what?" she replied, puzzled.

"I can't live a lie anymore. I tried, I really tried with David. But my heart isn't in it."

"Do you think it's because you've been spending so much time with Evan?"

"No, but when I'm with him, I..."

"You know it would be different if you were together," Susan countered. "Evan would become a *husband*. Not every moment would be fun and romantic."

"Susan, you don't understand. There is a place deep inside me. I don't know where it is. I can't find it on my own, but Evan knows where it is. It's a place only he can reach. No matter what David does, no matter how hard he tries, he can never reach it. I can try to fill it with other things—my shop, the house, distant hopes of children—but only Evan can fill it.

"It's not anything he says or does. It's just who he is. The completion of him. He walks inside me. Quietly, when I'm unaware. He doesn't say a word, doesn't look up. He walks right to the door, and I open freely. I am defenseless. But even when I am vulnerable, I feel safe.

"And when he is there, I am me. Anna Matthews. I am complete. Whole.

"For a long time, I pretended that place, that person no longer existed. I thought if I ignored it, it would go away and I could be content. Evan has opened that part of me again. If he leaves, I will be empty."

Anna was more descriptive of her love, and her need, for Evan than ever before. Susan could not argue these truths with her.

"But what about David? There are practical issues. You and David have a new house and..."

"Believe me, I've thought about it. It would be much easier to stay with David. I know I could have a comfortable life. I thought when we bought our house, we would begin building a life together—working on projects, making plans, sharing dreams. But we just ended up with more space. And I grew even lonelier.

"I know this is going to devastate him. He's never done anything to hurt me. But, I wouldn't want to spend my life with someone who stayed with me half-heartedly."

Anna spoke quickly, resolutely.

"What would it be like to live with him the next forty years always longing to be with Evan? If I left now, David would be young enough to find a woman who could give him her whole heart."

Anna's decision was apparent. She was summoning courage to proceed, hoping Susan would confirm her choice.

"If I wait, he will eventually discover that I have been living a lie for years. Susan, am I being selfish?"

"Do you want to know what I really think, Anna?"

"Yes, I do," she replied hesitantly.

"No, I do not think you are being selfish. I have watched you struggle. I am not one who says, 'do what is best for you.' *That* is selfish. It's not just about you—there are others involved. I don't know Evan. Honestly, I don't care about *his* feelings, except for the fact that you obviously love him. I do know David and he is the innocent one."

Anna looked down, feeling ashamed. Susan continued evenly.

"I believe in working hard to save your marriage. And you have done that. You could go to counseling, you could give it more time. But I don't think that would help. I think you made a mistake in marrying David in the first place."

"Do you really?" Anna was stunned. "Why didn't you ever say anything?"

"I never sensed you were confident in your decision to marry David, but I couldn't say anything then. I am not going to make that mistake again and I don't believe you should compound your first mistake by staying with him. I don't think you even have a choice. Your heart is not divided, Anna. Your heart belongs to Evan."

"Susan, I don't have any doubts about Evan. None. I only struggle with what will happen to David and..."

"Anna, ultimately he will find out that you are not his anymore. And if I were David, I would want to know sooner rather than later. How betrayed would you feel if you found out after five or ten years that your spouse didn't want to be with you? What did you say before? That you would be living a lie? That's not you, Anna."

"Hi, Evan!"

"Hey, Anna! How are you?"

"I'm fine. Did you have a good time in Boston?"

"The book signings went well. But it's good to be home. Have things settled down at the shop?"

"Yeah. But, I'm getting ready for Easter now."

An awkward silence.

"Anna, I miss you. A lot."

"I miss you, too, Evan," she replied.

Evan breathed a sigh of relief.

"Can I come see you tomorrow?" she asked.

An odd request, but judging by her tone, a good thing.

"Sure, but it's Saturday. How are you going to..."

"I can be there by noon. Will that be okay?"

"Of course. Is everything okay, Anna?"

"Yeah. I just want to see your home, where you write."

Evan knew it was more than that.

Anna drove up the winding gravel drive lined with evergreens and maples. She looked around and smiled. It fit Evan. Simple. Warm. Inviting. Expansive.

Evan had bought the house a year after returning from South America. He needed a new beginning away from his childhood home in Quechee. Built in the early 1800's, the small cape cod was striking against the backdrop of sweeping meadows and snowcapped green mountains. Its distinctive dormers and simplicity had attracted Evan. The house had been restored several times over the years to recapture its original charm. A creek stone wall bordered a front yard anchored by thick clusters of birches and evergreens. A stream wound its way through the back yard. Small dairy farms brushed his property's western edge while open fields spread toward the hills on the opposite side.

Evan ran outside to greet Anna, opening the door before her car had stopped. "I'm so glad you're here, Anna."

"I am, too." She stepped out of the car, gazing at the house. "Evan, it's beautiful."

Kirk Martin

"Thanks. But it needs a lot of work."
"Maybe needs a woman's touch?"
"Sure, but not just any woman."
She loved how they fell into easy, playful conversation.
Evan led her through the house. Anna absorbed every detail—the molding, woodwork and built-in bookcases that gave the house character. She lingered in the den.
"So this is where you write?"
"Yeah."
She noticed the soaring mountains. "What an inspiring view, Evan!"
He gazed at her with a sheepish grin. "The mountains are not my inspiration, Anna."
"That's sweet."
"Didn't say it to be sweet. Just true."
Anna sauntered over to Evan and wrapped her arms around his neck, smiling widely. "So, sweet man, want to show me what you've done with your great outdoors?"
"Hey, you just wait," he said, grabbing her hand. He pulled her down the hallway, giggling. A cool breeze greeted them on the porch. "See that stream? Dug it out myself."
"And I suppose you *make* and then *melt* the snow that feeds into it?" Anna replied sarcastically. They smiled at each other, enjoying the repartee.
"That's where I split firewood, down by the stream. And up there," he said, pointing to the bedroom window, "is where you would be watching me. Only you would think that I wouldn't notice. But I'd know."
"And do you know what I'd be thinking while I watched you do your manly chores?" she asked playfully.
"How amazed you are at the precision with which I split wood?"
"Of course." She was beaming.

166

Anna walked down the steps into his yard and twirled around, reveling in the expansive landscape.

"You know, we could do a lot with that area down by the stream," Evan began.

"Maybe we could create a sitting area. Border it with daisies and purple cone flowers and black-eyed susans. Maybe plant lilacs and baby's breath for crafting, too. We could sit out there and eat lunch together and..."

"And place lanterns all around so we could spend summer evenings listening to the brook, gazing up at the stars and..."

They were in their world again, creating scenes of life together, their expressions animated, descriptions flowing faster and faster.

"We could build a winding pathway and weave creeping thyme between the stones so we can smell the fragrance with every step. And..."

The fact that they were using possessive pronouns such as *our* and *we* did not go unnoticed.

"Hey, would you like a soda or some lemonade?" Evan offered.

"Lemonade would be great."

"Okay, I'll be right back."

Anna breathed in the fresh air. It was becoming real. They were going to do this. At home, David managed the lawn and shrubs while Anna took care of the flowers and decorating. Evan *and* Anna would make their plans together, arrange the stones together, plant the flowers together.

"Thanks," Anna said, taking the glass. "You know what I've always wanted outside my kitchen window?"

"What?" Evan replied, grinning widely.

"What are you laughing at?"

"I'm not laughing, just smiling. At you. I love the way you get excited about simple things. You know, like having a birdfeeder outside your kitchen window. I can see you..."

Anna hit Evan on the arm and pushed him away, his drink spilling. "How did you know?"

"Do you think I don't listen? I can see you in the kitchen watching happily as the little birds sing to you in the morning. And going out to make sure they have enough food, and buying special seed and..."

"Okay. Okay," Anna said, embarrassed by her transparency, elated at his understanding of her.

They strolled the property for the better part of the afternoon, talking and laughing. "Hey, you know what," Anna said, glancing at her watch. "I should be going."

They walked slowly to the porch and Evan opened the screen door. Anna motioned to the rocking chairs.

"Can we sit together for a few minutes?"

"Not yet."

"Why not?"

He leaned in to whisper. "I'm waiting for you, Anna."

A knowing smile lit her face. She looked down, almost blushing, before meeting his eyes in a long, silent gaze.

"I wish you didn't have to go, Anna. Seems like you just got here."

"I know," she said with resignation. "But I'll be back."

The day could have been better only if Anna had been able to stay. Some days she needed Evan's comfort, but today she needed his strength. Monday night, she would tell David. He would be angry and hurt, unable to understand. She would try to ease the shock, the pain while maintaining her resolve.

The anticipation of talking to David would be worse than the actual conversation. The truth would ease a heavy burden. Closing her eyes, she imagined the peaceful release in the safety of Evan's arms, their love finally complete.

Evan roamed the aisles of a hardware store and loaded gardening tools, topsoil, shrubs, mulch and seed into his truck. He found the perfect birdfeeder for Anna in a small craft store. Evan worked feverishly outside. As nightfall hovered, Evan continued working. Using outside floodlights and the high beams from his truck, he managed to clean up before surrendering to darkness.

Filthy and exhausted, he stood motionless under the hot shower, shoulders relaxed and head up, evaporating into the steam. Two hours later, he fell asleep by the warmth of the fire. Alone. Hoping it would be the last time.

Chapter 19

"I HAVE some good news, Anna. You're going to have a baby. Just experiencing some morning sickness, that's all. Congratulations!"

Anna felt as cold and sterile and lifeless as the examining room. In an instant, one life began and another ended.

Susan burst through the door, running to the back of the shop. Anna sat slumped on an old crate in the corner of the room, hair tangled, eyes swollen and red.

"Oh, my God, Anna, what's wrong?"

"I'm pregnant, Susan."

Anna sobbed.

"Shhhh. It's going to be okay. It's going to be okay." What else could she say? Susan hugged her for several minutes before she could speak.

Anna backed away, wiping her nose and tossing the tissue into a heap on the floor. "I've gotten myself into a big mess this time, haven't I?" she said, half-laughing, half-crying.

"Does David know? Evan?"

"No. I need to tell Evan in person. I want to tell David after I pull myself together."

"So you are going to stay with David?"

"I don't have a choice, do I? I can't let my mistake in marrying David affect an innocent life."

The day was a blur. The irony surreal. She had planned to tell David tonight that she was leaving, that their futures would be spent apart. Instead, she would inform him she was pregnant. And they would begin planning a new future together.

Anna considered waiting another two months before telling David and Evan to guarantee the pregnancy remained healthy. But she couldn't make Evan wait. The past few weeks had been too intense. She could not keep this secret. Even if she did, would she then find herself hoping for the unthinkable—a miscarriage—so she could be with Evan? She could not put herself in that position. Neither could she consider any other options. The decision had been made for her.

Evan had just climbed the steps of the back porch when he heard the phone ring. His boots were muddy from clearing brush along the stream, the melted snow leaving the ground soggy. He tugged his boots, letting them fall with a thud, and ran into the house, swiveling his body around the corner to grab the phone.

"Hello?"

"Hi, Evan. It's me."

"Hey, Anna!"

The enthusiasm in his voice drew her, but she couldn't give in. "I need to see you. Can I come down this afternoon?"

171

"Are you okay, Anna? Why don't I come see you? You were just…"

"No, I want to come there. It will take me a couple hours, okay?"

"Sure, Anna. I'll be here. Be careful."

"I will. Bye."

She gripped the counter and steadied herself.

Evan returned to his labors, excited to show Anna what he had accomplished—the birdhouse, the clearing for their sitting area.

Her voice sounded pale, but he attributed it to the circumstances. Maybe she told David last night. She would be drained, somber from ending a relationship. Evan never expected it to be easy.

Drained of emotion. That's what she sounded like.

Evan worked for another hour before eating and showering. He peered out the upstairs window, satisfied with his work.

I'll be back.

Her words sang.

The prospect of telling David she intended to leave was dreadful. Telling Evan their dream had ended *again* would be even worse.

Driving to his house, she considered the alternatives. But in her mind, she had no options. She had to stay with David. He was the father of the child she carried.

She couldn't have contact with Evan anymore. The connection would draw her away.

Already numb, she couldn't allow herself to think or feel—she had to say goodbye. She knew if she stayed long today, the force of emotion would overwhelm her convictions.

Anna heard the familiar crunching of small white stones and winced inside. As she neared the house, she saw Evan running to meet her. Oh, God, she thought, he is like a little kid. He must have a surprise for me. I can't do this to him.

"Hey, you made it pretty quickly. I'm glad you're here."

Before Anna could respond, Evan had taken her by the hand, leading her to the back yard over the stone path. "I want to show you something," he began. His eyes were alive. "Remember Saturday we talked about creating an area by the stream where we could sit in the evening and talk, and where you could have flower beds and where we..."

"Evan." Anna tried unsuccessfully to interrupt.

"...could have lunch on warm, sunny days in the..."

Anna couldn't let him go on. He drew pictures of a life that could never be.

"Evan. Evan." He stopped and peered at her intently, startled by the gravity in her voice.

"Evan, I'm pregnant."

Evan stared into the mountains. Anna turned away. She could not watch the life drain from him. All he had lived for was gone.

Evan mumbled, unable to speak. He didn't want to say anything inane, callous or selfish. He stepped toward Anna and enveloped her in his arms. They clung to each other.

No words were necessary.

Evan led her inside. Anna glanced around, snapping pictures of *their* house. Through the kitchen window, she spotted the birdfeeder. Pain pierced her heart.

She had to go.

"I will always love you, Evan. I have never stopped. I am so sorry, please..."

"Shhh. I know. I love you, Anna. God, I love you. You are the only..." His strength shattered.

Anna trembled. "Will you write to me, Evan?" She pleaded for a comforting assurance that *they* would continue, if only through his books.

He could only nod. The sound of his sobbing broke her. Anna collapsed into his arms, their faces together, his eyes looking deep into hers, tears intermingling and running down their chins, his hands stroking her hair, caressing her face, clutching her hands in a lingering touch, mouths open, taking in each other's warm breath for the last time.

"I miss you already, Evan," she whispered.

Anna turned and rushed out the door, down the steps and to her car. She started the engine and moved slowly down the drive, glancing back at Evan. Tears streamed. She pressed her hand flat against the glass, reaching for him.

Evan stood in the window, lips quivering, broken. He pressed his hand hard against the window, fingers spread widely, watching her move down the gravel drive away from him forever. He leaned against the window and buried his face in his arms, sobbing.

Anna was gone.

He stared through the cold, indifferent glass, the mountains and landscape that once seemed so boundless and full of promise closing in, trapping him like a prisoner inside his own house, inside his own soul. The snow was receding, revealing the stark reality of tree limbs, grass and fields left damp and desolate. Like him.

He could smell her perfume on his collar, and he was disoriented. He lifted his hand to the windowpane, watching her drive away again and again.

Now close the windows and hush all the fields:
If the trees must, let them silently toss;
No bird is singing now, and if there is,
Be it my loss.
                    - Robert Frost, *Now Close The Windows*

Chapter 20

THE DRENCHING April rain widened puddles scattered through the yard. All outdoors dwelt burdened and heavy— leaves, trees, pastures, wooden steps, even the sky, sodden. A clinging mist clothed the mountains, their peaks—like the sun—drowned in a dark, gray cloak. Evan rocked. The whispering hush of showers washed through the countryside, drops pattering off shingles. The rhythmic tap was broken by the sound of a car pulling up the driveway. The postman had already visited. Two cords of firewood were not due for another three weeks. Evan folded the paper on the table and pushed up with both arms, steadying himself against the rail before shuffling through the house. A hearty knock beat him to the door.

"Just a minute," he called out. "I'm coming."

Evan slid the throw rug from beneath the lip of the door with his foot and unlocked the dead bolt. He twisted the loose doorknob and pulled.

Something inside him stirred.

He squinted and adjusted his glasses, moving a step closer.

"Hi, Mr. Forrester. My name is Angela Helton. My mother is…" The woman stopped, distracted by his bewildered look. His eyes widened and then peered into her. He moved closer still. His mouth fell open.

With voice choked and heavy, he uttered her name.

"Anna."

Evan absorbed the wonder that had appeared in his doorway. He suddenly felt self-conscious, as if Anna faced him. They stood awkwardly, staring at each other, unsure what to say.

"How...how did you know?"

"Your face. Your eyes." Evan continued to absorb every detail, his heart racing, his mouth dry. "You shine like her."

His eyes, though worn, never doubted.

"Do you mind if I come in, Mr. Forrester?"

"Oh, of course, please do. It's a little messy."

He couldn't break his stare. She would be forty-two. She's a grown woman. Seems so young. Then again, everyone seemed young now. A little older than when he last saw Anna, her hair a shade lighter, shorter too. But the green eyes were a perfect match. Why was she here? How does Anna's daughter know about me?

"Please sit. Can I get you something to drink?"

His hands trembled. *He* needed to sit.

"No, I'm fine. Thank you." She walked into the living room, glancing about.

Evan sat in the chair. His head spun, mixing with images of Anna and her daughter. Longings and aches dulled with time suddenly became acute, piercing.

"How...how is your Mom?" he asked gently.

She sat on the end of the sofa, looking directly at him. "Well, that's why I needed to see you, Mr. Forrester."

Evan cringed, dreading the unthinkable. He would know when she passed away, he thought—he would sense the separation in his soul.

177

"My father passed away a year ago. I've spent a lot of time with Mom the past few months—going through her things, talking, getting ready to sell the house."

Angela paused and glanced away before looking at Evan. "Mom told me about you. About your relationship."

Evan shifted, wondering what she thought of him.

"At first, I thought she was being sentimental. You know, remembering a first love and making it out to be something it really wasn't. Then I read the books, Mr. Forrester. I know you love her."

Evan swallowed.

"My mom was diagnosed with breast cancer two years ago. She's a survivor. But fighting the cancer, along with old age, has left her body weak." Angela took a deep breath. "Mom has lived her entire life for others. I don't know if she has one year or twenty left, but I have one wish. I want her to be happy. When she talks about you, I see something in her I've never seen. Her eyes are alive, her voice filled with affection. The only thing she wants is you."

Angela paused and spoke softly to him.

"You need to be together, Mr. Forrester."

Evan shifted again, attempting to cover his involuntary shudder. This is happening too fast. First, Anna appears in my doorway. Angela, rather. Now she is saying Anna needs me. "But what…" he stuttered, unable to express himself.

"I know it's a lot to ask, and Mom doesn't know I am here. But I've read the books," she said, a cheery smile chasing away tears, "and I think I know you pretty well, Mr. Forrester. I believe you want the same thing."

He felt unsure of himself, afraid he could not give Anna what she needed. "I'm seventy-four now, an old man. Are you sure she'd still want me?"

"Have *you* ever stopped needing *her*?"

Evan stood and motioned to her. "Come with me, Angela."

She followed. He did not seem frail anymore. In the presence of someone so close to Anna—someone who understood their connection—hope returned. He strode spryly and purposefully toward his den. Angela stepped through the French doors, gazing at the bookshelves, desk and fireplace. Dozens of novels bearing the name Jackson lined the shelves. Angela was moved by the thought that her mom had stood here forty-some years ago, in love with this man.

She remained so.

Angela was beginning to see why. She noticed the lone photograph resting on Evan's desk. He picked it up with care, holding it with both hands. He moved alongside her and spoke tenderly.

"This is your Mom when she was twenty-years-old, out at Cynthiana Gorge."

Angela glanced up at him as he spoke about Anna, telling stories from their days together at the Gorge, revering the picture, adoring her mom.

She heard what her mom had heard in his voice. She saw what her mom had seen in his eyes.

"I love your Mom, Angela. I…"

"I know, Mr. Forrester."

"I just don't want to disappoint her."

"She loves you."

She's Anna's girl, alright. Confident. Purposeful.

They hugged, grasping a common connection.

"Will you please consider what I've said today, Mr. Forrester?" She placed a piece of paper with Anna's phone number and address in his hand and smiled. "She needs you."

He lifted his hand again to the windowpane, his fingers clearing a streak from the glass. The damp, cool beads of condensation hung on his fingertips as he watched Anna's daughter drive away.

Chapter 21

CLAPPING THUNDER fractured the sky, rolling west to east through the heavens. Spreading rumble, building louder until cracking again, followed dull booms. The house shook, windows shuddered. Sharp flashes sliced the evening sky, lighting a world beyond the mountains. Evan turned from the window to face the rows of books neatly stacked one after another. They chronicled the past half-century like still frames of his life with Anna. At least as they had imagined.

You need to be together.

His first instinct was to go immediately. But something held him back. Was it fear? Comfort? He had grown comfortable loving Anna from a distance—through words in books, safely detached from genuine emotional engagement. The sting of separation became a part of life. Writing soothed the ache.

But being with Anna would leave him exposed, vulnerable to emotions capable of leaving fresh scars. If he remained alone, he could continue writing letters to her, carrying to the grave an unmatched love.

Have you ever stopped needing her?

No, he hadn't. But would she really feel the same? He wasn't the same young man she fell in love with. He was old, wrinkled, thin. His stories proceeded slowly. He fumbled thoughts and forgot important details.

What if being together fell short of their expectations? Wouldn't it be better to leave the dream untainted? It is perfect now, unblemished by imperfections, safe from certain anguish. Death would visit, loneliness would return.

Questions and doubts and longings swirled. Evan lived a simple life, unaccustomed to making difficult decisions. He sought refuge in his chair overlooking the limitless landscape.

A cool breeze swept clouds toward the Atlantic. The sun appeared briefly before descending over the horizon, a faint rainbow arching above the mountains. Crickets chirped in the grass, the lawn turning dark with night. Evan surveyed his yard, thinking about the day, about Anna, about Angela. Right there below him. Forty-three years ago. He was showing Anna the garden and sitting area.

She told him she was pregnant. With Angela. The same girl who now wanted to bring them together.

I'm too old for this, he thought.

He glanced over at the empty chair creaking in the wind—and made his decision.

Water sloshed from the bucket onto the floor, trickling in rivulets along the hardwood grooves. Evan pushed the mop through the kitchen, wondering where all the dirt had come from. He had thoroughly scrubbed every cupboard, drawer and utensil tray until everything was spotless. Except for the small round coffee stains indelibly specking the counter. He hadn't used most of these muscles in years. He wondered if he needed more pots and pans. The refrigerator looked barren.

He shuffled piles of magazines, newspapers and catalogs from spot to spot. They didn't belong anywhere, except the ballooning trash bag. He had stuffed three already this morning. And he hadn't rummaged through closets yet. He tidied the living room, fluffing pillows, refolding the quilt draped over the sofa, dusting tables and lampshades. He labored meticulously through every room, stuffing bag after bag until completing the first floor. He generally kept the house orderly, but women noticed everything. And Anna was not just any woman.

Shortly after noon, he fixed a sandwich and enjoyed lunch on the porch. He looked at the chair, imagining how wonderful it would feel to sit next to her. The excitement that raced through him as a young man surged again. Love and passion knew no age. He imagined the conversations they would have, wondered what her skin would feel like. Could he still feel the magic through his wrinkled skin?

Evan rose from the chair, cleaned his dishes and found his car keys. He traced the path of his morning walk, coasting past Otter Creek Falls to find a space close to the barbershop. It had ceased to be a barbershop a few years prior—the revolving candy stripe a memory—but men didn't visit hair salons, did they?

"Hey, old man!" Evan shouted to the man easily twenty years his junior. His name was Tony Simonini. Slightly round, short, with jet-black hair greased back on either side. He wore a permanent smile and a gregarious nature. The creases in his olive skin gave away his Italian heritage. As did his name and penchant for good wine and pasta.

"What brings you back in here so soon?" Tony replied, glancing up while shaving a man's beard.

"Just need a little trim."

"What little is sprouting out of that head of yours, I'd keep if I were you," the barber replied with a hearty chuckle.

Evan took a seat against the wall, enjoying the banter. "You can only hope you'll have such gorgeous locks when you're my age," Evan snapped back.

The barber applied a hot towel to the clean-shaven face and allowed the gentleman to appreciate his work through a small mirror. He snapped the smock off the man and welcomed Evan to the chair. Standing behind him, running the black comb through Evan's gray strands, Tony began snipping.

"You got yourself a date or something?" he asked.

Evan never could hide his affection for Anna.

Translucent droplets reflecting golden rays slid down long blades of grass. Bluebirds and wrens hunted worms hiding beneath the soil, flying back to nests hidden by budding leaves. Squirrels scampered through damp woods and abruptly stopped, standing alert on hind legs. Evan strolled by with his morning paper. He had stayed up past midnight cleaning the upstairs. His legs—actually his entire body—ached from cleaning. He had scratched off nearly every item on his list. Hair trimmed. House cleaned. Refrigerator and cupboards filled. Only one item remained.

Anna.

He wondered if she would come. He considered the possibility that their time would be limited, but his life would be incomplete without her.

Evan spread the paper on the kitchen table and forced down a piece of toast. After breakfast, he showered and shaved, searching the medicine cabinet and linen closet for aftershave. He found cologne and slapped it across his face, forgetting how it burned. He looked in the mirror, wondering if Anna would like what she saw.

Searching his closet, he slid on his best khaki trousers and a striped, blue button-down. He found a burgundy belt, something he had not worn in years, and slipped on matching loafers. He returned to the bathroom, slightly hunched, his eyes inches from the mirror, searching to make sure he hadn't missed anything. One more brush through his hair— the part had to be just right. One more examination of the house, straightening towels and beds and linens.

He trotted to his car, feeling like a high school boy about to pick up his girl.

Evan passed through impressive gates. Sprawling homes sat on top of each other in perfect rows. Evan looked down at the piece of paper scrunched in his hand. 1354 Southwick Lane. He turned left at the stop sign and coasted down the quiet street. 1360. 1358. His heart beat faster and insides knotted. Feelings unfamiliar to an old man. 1356. A hard swallow. 1354. He drove past once. How could he not be ready? He had waited his entire life for this opportunity. He turned around at the corner and stopped in front of the house, straining at the windows for a peek at Anna. Vivid images flashed through his mind. The first time he saw her in the bookstore. The way she smiled and laughed, their walks to her car, the day at the Gorge, long rides together, holding hands, leaving her, returning to find her with another man, a few weeks of bliss during a hopeful winter forty-three years ago.

He turned into the driveway and climbed slowly out of the car, glancing up at the windows, wondering if she had seen him. He shuffled among daisies and tulips lining the walk.

He cleared his throat and ran his hand through his hair. The doorbell clanged loudly. He stood for a long moment, shifting weight from one leg to the other, hands fidgeting. He rang again. What if she isn't...

The door opened.

He didn't see the wrinkles, didn't see the lines or the gray hair.

He looked into her eyes and saw his past, his present, his future. He saw love and grace and beauty.

He knew he was going to see her today, but he was not adequately prepared. A lifetime of longing and yearning merged into one moment. Changing his life once again. Tears seeped from his eyes as the lump in his throat grew larger still.

"Hello, Anna."

She could not answer, only move toward him. She swore if she had the chance, she would never let go.

He delighted in the way the contours of her body remained so perfect against his. He grasped her tightly and stroked her hair, still soft. Only the color had changed.

He whispered something restrained for too long—words expressed on paper, but not spoken. Slowly. From his own mouth. To her.

"I've missed you, Anna."

She groaned and sobbed into his chest. Her body fell limp into his arms, her strength gone.

"Maybe we should go inside," he said softly, patting her back. "You don't want the neighbors talking, do you?"

She backed up, laughing through sniffles, and gazed into his eyes again. Her expression turned serene, deliberate. She closed her eyes and moved slowly into him until she felt the soft, light impress of his lips against hers. She sank into him and vanished. His face was warm against her skin, his body sure next to hers. She lingered in him for a moment, before looking deeply into him, their faces together, hands now clutching. His fingers stroked her hair, now her face.

"What are you doing here, Evan?" she breathed.

He pulled her closer and spoke softly. "I heard a voice whispering, 'Go get your angel before she flies away.' Will you come home with me, Anna?"

Home.

She had lived in many houses, but she had never been home. She melted into him, hoping his warmth would dissolve her fears.

"Evan, I...I don't..."

"Why are you unsure, Anna? Isn't this what we have always wanted, a chance to be together?"

She stepped back and looked down. "Look at me, Evan. I am an old woman. I am weak. I don't know how long I have."

He swallowed. "Anna, I..."

"I don't want to hurt you again. All these years, I have regretted how much pain I caused..."

"Anna, that's not true. You didn't do anything to hurt..."

"Evan, I have known the greatest love a woman could ever know. A man spent his life writing love letters to me— while I moved on with my life and he remained alone. I have known your love every day. You have given me your whole life. I have given you nothing."

"All I ever wanted was to be with you. And now we have that chance."

"But I don't want to hurt you, Evan."

"The only way you can hurt me is if you don't come. We can't miss this opportunity, Anna. Besides, I spent a hundred dollars on that rocking chair and it's never been used."

Evan had walked through that door. He was roaming inside again.

She couldn't say no.

Chapter 22

ANNA WATCHED Evan heave the suitcases into the trunk. She was seventy-two-years-old and just beginning to live a dream she had held in her heart since she was twenty. A young girl with a ponytail in a college bookstore. Now her hair was gray, her arms, hands and face wrinkled and pale.

She sat in the sedan next to Evan, feeling like a giddy schoolgirl. "That daughter of mine came to see you, didn't she?"

"I don't know what you mean, Anna." His smile. His endearing smile. Through the creases, it still spoke to her.

"What did she tell you?"

"That you still loved me," he replied whimsically.

She had grown accustomed to feeling frail physically. But not emotionally. And now she was collapsing inside. She looked at him. Gray haired, thin, aged. But he spoke like a little boy. *That you still loved me.* His tone and inflection. It's still all he cared about—all he needed.

Anna put her arm through his and grasped his forearm with both hands. She gently stroked his arm as they drove. The memories flooded back. His dark hairs tickling her fingers, the way his thumb caressed her skin when they held hands.

"She's just like you, Anna. Beautiful. Determined."

"She's a good girl. She was the only thing that held me together."

They talked for the next hour about Angela and her family. They spoke more slowly, but he still made her laugh. Something she had not done in a long time. Anna noticed a change in her voice, a change inside. She felt alive. Playful. Complete.

As they neared the house, their anticipation grew. Anna sat forward, staring out the window. Through the maples and birches budding with spring, she saw the house. The crunching gravel welcomed her.

The sun cast long shadows across the front yard. Rolling up the driveway felt like slow motion, years of hopes and dreams coming into focus. She was here to stay. Not for a night. Not for a visit. For the rest of her life.

"I hope you aren't disappointed. I've tried to keep up with everything, but it's still missing your touch." He scooted around the car to open her door.

She patted his arm as she stared at the house, strolling the sidewalk. He helped her up the steps. The same steps she had left behind four decades ago. Then her legs had bounce. Their bodies had changed, but the feelings inside remained the same.

Evan opened the door. "I'd try to carry you over the threshold, Anna, but I'm afraid we'd end up a heap of old bones on the floor."

"Just hold my hand, Evan."

They shuffled through the front door. Anna looked around, faded snapshots mixing with the present.

He leaned and whispered in her ear. "Welcome home, Anna."

She squeezed his hand. They felt a little awkward, not knowing how to begin this new life. But she had walked through the door and she was not going to leave without him. Ever.

Evan led her through the house to the back porch. The screen door creaked open and slammed behind them.

"We've waited a long time, Anna."

He pulled her rocking chair close to his. She eased into the chair. They rocked in silence as Anna reached for his hand. He had wondered whether he could still feel the electricity through coarse, wrinkled skin. Now he knew.

She glanced at a small table. Cheerful daisies sprang from a vase. He remembered. A gentle, unspoken reminder. What was that word she had felt as a young woman?

Blissful.

"You still have magic in those hands, Anna?"

"If I have the right inspiration."

"I could sure use some help along the stream. The sitting area could use your touch. It's sort of bare, you know."

"I'm sure we can make it beautiful." Being together seemed to wake passions dormant for years. "I miss the feel of the dirt."

"Well, you don't think I brought you here to relax, do you? I'm putting you to work, granny."

"Will you get dirty with me?"

"I thought you'd never ask."

They smiled and talked about the flowers they would plant, much as they had one special Saturday afternoon. The sun began its descent, cool air rode in on afternoon clouds. Reluctantly, they climbed from their chairs to get Anna settled.

Evan followed her as they walked through the back door. "It was worth the wait, you know." He heard her smile, felt her pat his leg.

Evan lugged the suitcases up the stairs step by step. Halfway to the top, he leaned against the railing, catching his breath. "You planning on staying awhile or something?" he kidded.

"You're not getting rid of me, Mister."

Reaching the hallway, Evan looked at her seriously. "I wasn't sure where you wanted to sleep and I didn't want to be presumptuous. So I prepared a room just for you."

He clicked on the light to a quaint room. Anna peeked in, delighting in the dainty accents. Fresh flowers bloomed in the windowsill. Small, framed pictures of birds and an antique mirror adorned the walls. A crystal lamp rested on a white, lace doily atop the nightstand.

She decided that he was a cute old man. Cute as he was as a young man. She was glad time had not changed him. He had not grown bitter, had not lost his passion.

"Where do *you* want me to sleep, Evan?"

"Well, I forgot to mention that this is a deluxe room here at the Forrester Inn. It will cost you seventy-five dollars a night. And you have to make your own bed. Now there is one place at the Inn where you can sleep free."

He could not contain his smile.

"And where would that be?" she inquired.

"Where no one else has ever been. In my arms."

A tear escaped as she nestled next to him. "Good, I want you to hold me and never let go."

They shared a kiss and continued down the hallway, Evan dragging the suitcase. "Lovely little room there, though," he muttered, proud of his work.

Breathtaking mountains and fields and stream played through the bedroom windows. Evan showed Anna her closet before retrieving the rest of her belongings.

She stood in the closet, busily hanging blouses and pants, talking loudly so Evan could hear from the other room. She turned to find more hangers.

"Evan! How long have you been standing there?"

"Just for a minute. By the way, you don't have to speak so loudly. My hearing isn't *that* bad."

She waved her hand, shooing him away.

"Do you know how long I have waited to watch you hang clothes, see you appear from behind a closed door, hear your footsteps on the floor? Besides, you broke the number one rule of the house."

She looked at him warily. "And what rule would that be?"

"The two-inch rule."

"And what is the two-inch rule?" she asked dryly.

"Ha! I can't believe you don't know what the two-inch rule is." He shook his head, muttering, "What have I gotten myself into here?"

She stared at Evan, unsure whether he was irritating or adorable—or perhaps both.

"Anna, the first rule of the house is that we can never be more than two inches apart," he said, pausing. "Otherwise, I will be lonely."

Anna dropped the blouse and sauntered over to Evan, placing her arms around his neck. "In that case, why don't we make it a no-inch rule?"

Evan held her, savoring the touch and warmth. Minutes passed quickly. Even as they released, they held each other's gaze, amazed at reality.

Evan's expression turned serious. "You know, if you're going to leave your clothes on the floor, we may have some problems."

Anna swatted Evan's arm and turned to finish unpacking. She looked up mischievously. "I have a few rules, too, you know."

"Like what?"

"Like I do all the cooking."

"Well, can't argue with you there. That *is* in your own best interest."

They walked down the stairs to the kitchen. Birds gathered at the feeder. Evan put his arms around her as they watched together. Together. It was strange, wonderful, natural.

"Why don't I fix dinner?" Anna opened the refrigerator, aghast. She closed the door and searched the pantry and cupboards. "Evan, don't you keep any food in this house?"

"I just went shopping yesterday and stocked up on everything."

"No wonder I can see right through you! I'm going to put some meat on those bones if it's the last thing I do." She pinched Evan and continued searching the kitchen for pots, pans and food enough to scrape together a meal.

She was taking care of him. He liked it. And so did she.

Safe. She hadn't felt like this in over forty years. Her head rested on Evan's chest, wrapped in his arms.

She listened to his heart beat.

She felt him opening that door and walking into the deep place inside her. Only now he wouldn't have to leave.

She exhaled, years of tension and holding back moving to complete surrender. She could give herself with abandon.

She was exhausted. Emotionally charged and drained at the same time. She resisted thoughts of lost opportunities, content to enjoy every moment.

He recalled the countless nights he crawled into bed alone. Cold. Unfeeling. An empty bed in a sea of space. He woke through the night to listen to her breathe.

Not knowing she was awake. Listening to him breathe.

They were in love.

Madly.

Chapter 23

A GENTLE tease of wind blew sweet clover through the valley. The countryside slowly flushed with tints of green, fields and meadows dappled with wildflowers blooming yellow, red, purple and pink. Birds chirped happily, honeybees skimming flowers hunting pollen. Reflections of a warming sun danced lightly across the crystal clear stream swollen with fresh rains. Baby cardinals climbed warily out of their nest perched atop the rough, wooden beam above the back porch. They sat side-by-side, scrawny bodies eclipsed by gaping yellow beaks.

Evan and Anna rocked slowly, the warm breeze playing a melody on the wind chimes. Their first morning together.

The sun began its ascent over the mountain peaks. High, lofty clouds drifted in and dispersed into wisps of air. All they noticed was the comforting presence of each other. It was for this they had waited.

The years had stolen a lifetime of conversations. Yet they felt no need to fill the silence. They *had been* together, lived a lifetime inside their own minds. Evan's books had created scenes they could enjoy, intimate moments to share. As if they had actually happened.

◆ ◆ ◆

"Need a little bit of topsoil right here, Evan," Anna said.

He knelt alongside and spread rich, black dirt into a small mound. Anna sculpted it with care, filling around flowers. They had been to the garden center earlier to pick up topsoil, seeds and plants. Their first errand together. Magic.

Anna dressed in old jeans and one of Evan's shirts. He wore khaki shorts and an old golf shirt with a baseball cap that looked as if Babe Ruth had rounded the bases in it. The same way he looked the first time she saw him. They concentrated on their work, occasionally stealing glances and kisses. They played in the soil all afternoon, stopping to drink lemonade in the grass.

Together.

Anna steadied herself on Evan's arm and rose to walk inside for a refill. Evan stared. Even in old age, she was stunning. The way she moved. She had not changed. Anna knew she was being watched. And she reveled in it.

"Hey," came a shout, "you're breaking the two-inch rule!"

Anna stopped and turned around. "So what is my punishment?"

Evan continued digging, looking down. "That is the punishment, Anna," he replied softly.

She felt something stir inside, a flutter in her stomach, the way it feels when driving fast over a steep hill. She turned, speechless, and continued to the house. She made a fresh pitcher of lemonade while enjoying the birds at the feeder.

When she returned, she heard a loud groan. Anna looked up and saw Evan writhing in pain, his body contorted in the dirt. The pitcher crashed to the ground. Anna ran as fast as she could. Oh, God, please don't let him die. We just got started. Sickness gripped her stomach as she fell to the ground by his side. He cringed.

"Evan! Evan! Are you okay? What is it? Is it your heart?"
"I think I did it this time, Anna."
"What? Evan?" she asked frantically. "Should I call nine-one-one?"
"Heavens, no!" He rolled to his side and clutched his lower back. "I think I threw my back out."
"Are you sure it's not your heart. Sometimes the pain can start..."
"No, I'm, okay. Really. I didn't mean to startle you. It's just my back."
"How did you hurt it?"
He sat up, still grimacing. "Well, that big rock was in the way," he began, pointing. "I wanted to move it, you know, to turn you on with my manliness."
Anna burst out laughing. "You silly man!" She leaned in and kissed him. "You turn me on just by being you."
"I guess I'm not the incredible physical specimen I used to be, huh?" he said, shaking his head.
"More so." Anna glimmered.

Anna and Evan welcomed each morning in their rocking chairs. Cardinals and bluebirds and wrens and hummingbirds greeted them. Afterward, they walked into town or worked in the garden before the summer heat ruled the day. Lazy afternoons were reserved for short drives into the country or reading books in the shade. They stayed active, but occasionally enjoyed a catnap. In the evening, they sat by the stream, admiring their efforts in the garden. And each other.

It seemed as if they had been together a lifetime—because they had been in many ways. Yet the newlywed feeling persisted, the thrill of discovery complemented by the completeness of friendship.

Chapter 24

THE AFTERNOON sun cast long shadows across the grass. Trees swayed gently in the warm breeze, the light filtering through full branches. Thin gray clouds swept across the sky quickly under slower moving, dense white masses. Flickering shadows gave way to shade as the clouds enveloped the sun.

Anna looked up from her book. "Evan, do you know what tomorrow is?"

"Thursday."

"The date, I mean."

"Well, what's today?"

"The twenty-sixth."

"Then I imagine tomorrow is May twenty-seventh."

She frowned. "Okay, mister smarty-pants. Very funny. Do you remember why that date is special?"

"I think that was the day Roger Clemens threw a no-hitter for the Sox against the Yankees a few years back." Evan smiled and looked straight at Anna. "And it was also the day I fell in love with you."

Her heart fluttered again. Just hearing him say those words. Even now. "You remembered!"

"It's not everyday you see an angel," he said softly.

She leaned over and kissed him, lingering near his lips. "I want to go up there. To the Gorge. And sit on our rock."

"Are you sure? It's a pretty strenuous hike. Especially for us geezers."

"I can do it." She paused and cocked her head. "Can *you* do it?"

She was not referring to his physical stamina. His body was stronger than hers. But, they would have to take an established trail, something Evan had *always* refused to do.

"Don't worry about me. I don't want you to overdo."

"I'll be fine."

"Okay, let's go in the morning before it gets too hot."

The dirt lot at the gorge overlook had been paved. New maps marked established trails. They stepped out of the car and breathed in sweet lilac and honeysuckle. Anna remained nervous about Evan following the established trails. She wanted this to be perfect. As it had been. They paused for a moment, letting their emotions settle.

Evan grabbed Anna's hand, bypassing the trail chart. She began to question, but she trusted him. He continued to his trail. Anna stopped suddenly.

"Well, are you coming?" he asked.

An oval sign on a weathered post stood next to the opening. Wildflowers bloomed all around. Anna read the words etched into wood.

> Welcome to Cynthiana Gorge.
> Where Angels sit on rocks
> And heaven meets earth.

"Evan?!" She hadn't even made it to the rock yet, and was crying. A lifetime of books. Now this.

She didn't ask questions, just tried to stop the tears as she took his hand and followed. He had not said anything about the sign or the trail. His path was not overgrown. He had never taken another's path.

Reds, purples, vibrant yellows and blues exploded around their feet. They were a blur to Anna. A short distance into the trail, they leaned against the hollowed-out trunk of a fallen tree. The bark stripped easily from decay. Squirrels scampered through the undergrowth and up trees, birds called from the canyon.

"You okay?" he asked, offering her water.

"I can't believe you." She shook her head, still wiping her eyes.

A slight smile escaped him. "I've come to know the Park Rangers over the years. I asked them if I could put that sign up." He paused for a moment, looking around. "You ready to keep moving? I've cleared out the trail, too, should be easier than…"

"I love you, Evan Forrester."

She leaned in and kissed him. He reached down and took her hands. They kissed again, soft, sweet. He stroked her cheek and hair. He kissed her lips, then her nose, her forehead, her cheek.

"I adore you, Anna," he whispered.

They embraced and leaned against the tree trunk, gazing up through the umbrella of green and brown, spotting brilliant patches of sky.

"We could just stay here, you know," he said.

She patted his leg and they resumed their hike, resting twice more before the clearing unfolded. Her anticipation grew with the roar of whitewater. She stepped from the forest and a warm breeze swept through her hair. The expanse enveloped her, the soaring air breathing new life into her—she felt like a little girl again. They made their way to the rock. The magnificence of the trees and canyon and whitewater surrounded them. It was like they were sitting on a precipice overlooking the earth, just the two of them spiraling above, absorbing its grandeur. They soaked in the sun, catching glances of each other and laughing.

"Evan, did you ever get tired of writing the books?"

"No. I needed a lifetime and every page to express my love for you. The images were endless."

"Sometimes, I felt as if they were real. I lived every scene, every story."

"Well, I guess my dream came true, didn't it? I don't need to write anymore."

They marveled at the gorge below. Birds soared, a comforting hush played through swaying trees. Anna longed to hear a story. Evan began slowly.

"Fifty-three years ago today, a young boy visited this canyon to admire what heaven had created. Little did he know that God had sent a creation so lovely she shone brighter than the sun. When the young boy beheld that wonder, he knew he had tasted of heaven—he had seen an angel. That angel stole his heart and never returned it. And he never asked for it back.

"The boy changed and grew into a man. Every week, he came to this rock, wondering if he would ever see her again. The man is old now and though his eyesight is failing, he knows she is an angel. She still shines brighter than the sun, her face glows with grace not common to man. And the man's heart beats faster when she is near.

"He always hoped an angel would consider marrying a mere man."

His hands trembled as he reached into his pocket and opened a small box.

"Anna, will you be my bride?"

Anna looked at him in awe. He was no mere man.

Strong and assured, an accomplished man who followed his own path and remained true to it. A giddy little boy, still full of wonder and joy unspoiled by the cares of the world. A frail old man, broken in body and spirit.

All magically wrapped into one.

Her Evan.

Raindrops leapt off the roof, soaking into the wooden steps below. Tiny green leaves flinched as droplets splashed on the azaleas bordering the porch. The rain pinged against gutters and gushed out of downspouts. A bubbling gully flowed to the stream.

Sandwich plates dotted with crumbs and a lone glass with milk streaking the sides remained on the table. Evan and Anna reminisced, recalling a snowy night at the college many winters ago.

Anna turned away, but Evan heard her tears.

"What's the matter, Anna?"

"I'm so sorry, Evan. I couldn't give you the best years of my life. My body is weak. My skin is wrinkled and pale. We can't travel like we had planned. We've missed so much. I wanted to…"

Evan squeezed her hand and gazed through her tears. "Anna, this is all I ever wanted."

Anna saw peace and serenity in eyes that were genuine.

She knew his calm assurance.

Chapter 25

A COOL September breeze swept through the bedroom window. A large, full moon cast its glow through the maples and birches, slivers of light illuminating angular parts of the floor and walls. Evan felt Anna trembling, her head buried in his chest.

"What's the matter, sweetheart?"

Anna did not respond, gripped by fear, unsure whether to reveal her thoughts. But she had never kept secrets from him.

"I'm scared, Evan."

He held her more tightly. "What are you afraid of?"

"My father told us that before my mom died, she could feel her body slipping away. I can feel it, Evan. I'm about to fly away." Anna sobbed in his arms. "I'm not ready to go yet, Evan. I want more time."

He kissed her head, but she could feel him holding back tears.

The crisp air returned as emerald peaks turned every imaginable hue of red, yellow, orange and gold. Buckets of freshly picked apples and sweet cider flooded roadside stands. Country fairs sprang up in quaint villages all over

Vermont. Bales of hay and scarecrows dotted fields stretching to the horizon in seas of orange. Large, red wagons bulging with pumpkins bumped along country roads. Leaves trickled from their perches, drifting down in a lonely dance.

Evan and Anna sensed their time was ending. They tried to pack a lifetime of memories and experiences into their remaining days. They took long walks, rocked for hours and never left each other's side. They observed the no-inch rule Anna had joked about. When she showered, Evan sat on the vanity and talked. They fixed every meal together, napped together. And worked outside together.

"You up for some yard work today, Anna?"

"It does feel good out here."

"Why don't we rake the leaves and prune a bit?"

They walked inside and set their dishes in the sink before making their way to the bedroom. They both put on jeans and boots. Anna buttoned one of Evan's old flannel shirts, sleeves rolled underneath the way he had always done. She liked to breathe in his scent—imagine she was *wearing* him. Evan pulled a navy blue Canterbury College sweatshirt over his head.

"How come you look better in my clothes than I do?" he asked.

"Probably because I am so much better looking than you," she replied, tickling his side.

"Don't make me chase you, little girl. I may have lost a step or two—okay, maybe a city block—but I'll get you!"

She waited at the top of the stairway, clasping his hand and kissing him on the cheek.

They strolled to the shed, grabbing work gloves and rakes. They began at the edges of the property and worked their way toward the center, leaving small piles scattered across the yard. The mix of exercise and cool air was refreshing. They stopped often to stretch their backs, leaning against trees and talking.

As the sun began its descent behind the mountains, ten piles dotted the yard. Only tiny parched fragments of leaves remained clustered between blades of combed grass.

"Want to get something to drink before cleaning up?" Evan asked.

"Sure. I could use a break."

They rested rakes against the stout maple and traipsed inside. Anna grabbed two glasses and Evan retrieved the pitcher from the refrigerator.

"Mmm. You smell like the outdoors." Anna sniffed Evan's sweatshirt. "I love that scent. Leaves and grass and autumn air."

"I know how we can both smell like that even more." He set his glass on the counter and pulled Anna toward the door. "Come on, before it gets too chilly."

Evan marched directly to his rake. He furiously heaved the piles together into one large, colorful mound underneath the maple. With each stroke, leaves fluttered into the air, teetering in somersaults before settling one on top of another. He worked his way around the edges of the mound, pulling stray leaves up to the peak.

He rested his rake against the maple, out of breath, and looked at Anna expectantly. She saw the young man she fell in love with.

She remained wildly in love.

"Are you ready?"

His hand was warm against a cool afternoon. She felt his heart pulse through his fingers. They took a few steps back. The damp pile of leaves gathered before them. Grassy fields with deep red barns and farmhouses lie beyond.

They turned and looked into each other's eyes. Destiny played the long reel of their life apart, their life together— snapshots and images spliced into a moving picture culminating in this moment.

Their legs danced above the earth for a final time, prancing across grass moist with encroaching dusk. The breeze became a strong current in their faces, faster they ran toward the beckoning leaves. Their hands melded into one. They squeezed tight and leapt with abandon, their bodies twisting in the air, shouts of glee echoing through the countryside.

They landed in the springing cushion of leaves pressed together. Leaves tumbled and toppled, clinging to their legs, arms, faces and necks. When they opened their eyes, they rested next to each other. In the shade of the maple. Reflections from a fading sun filtered through branches. Beyond distant peaks, shades of red and pink played behind dark clouds silhouetted against a pale blue sky.

Evan struggled for balance in the shifting mound. He moved closer, hovering over Anna. Her eyes were wide with wonder, glistening in the twilight, fixed beyond the sunset. She was twenty again. Graceful. Radiant.

He spoke softly in her ear. "I love my angel."

The cool air brushing across her skin still moist with the touch of his lips sent shivers through her body. She smiled serenely and gazed deeply into him. "I love my Evan."

They were the last words he heard her speak.

Chapter 26

THE HOUSE stared through him. It had grown accustomed to the patter of four footsteps. It had become full. Full of clothes, food, substance. Full of laughing and joy and conversation. Full of love.

Now it was empty. Cold. Lonely.

Death proved more painful than a lifetime of separation.

He had spent his life living for the promise of the future. Now he was grasping for a past beyond his reach.

He settled into the den. Robert Frost and a crackling fire returned as loyal companions.

> I dwell in a lonely house I know
> That vanished many a summer ago,
> And left no trace but the cellar walls,
> And a cellar in which the daylight falls,
> And the purple-stemmed wild raspberries grow...
>
> I dwell with a strangely aching heart
> In that vanished abode there far apart
> On that disused and forgotten road...
> - *Ghost House*

Evan closed the book. The words of another man would not suffice. No one could know what he felt. He picked up a pen and wrote his final words to Anna.

The house is no longer empty. Neither am I.
It is filled with memories. So am I.

I feel the bed lift slightly when you arise in the night. I hear you tiptoe across the floor. I am at peace when the bed dips again.

I see you smile while you make my sandwich. I know you hate peanut butter and jelly. You walk toward me with contentment playing on your lips. You eat your sandwich with me and do not complain.

We share a glass of milk and I leave you the last sip. You shake the crumbs from my lap. I am messy on purpose, you know. I like your touch. I like your attentiveness.

I like the way you reach up and pick lint off my shirt, your hand resting warm against my chest. I lean in and feel the softness of your hair sweeping across my skin and smell your fragrance.

I put the lint there.

I wake in the still of the night to gaze at you when you are unaware, awed by your grace and beauty. I waited fifty years. Sleep holds no allure, only you.

I hear the chair rock next to me. It no longer creaks. It moves across the planks with a dull thud, weighted by life. I know you are next to me. I feel content. Safe. Happy. Alive.

My hand searches for yours. I am relieved when I feel your warmth. I hear you laugh and I am whole.

I feel your gaze when I speak. I talk slower, longer. I feel complete in your eyes.

Five months. Fourteen days. I am tempted to think about all that we missed. The dreams of our youth. Our baby boy and girl. Vacations and experiences and chores never shared. A lifetime of hugs and kisses and conversations and laughs.

Fate left us frail bodies and time measured in days. Some would say fate cheated us. I say we were blessed with the greater gift. Weak bodies kept us from straying far. We had no distractions, save each other. I could wish for nothing more.

Did we not cherish every word, every syllable, every breath?

Did we not etch in our hearts every glimmer, every tear, every laugh?

Did we not treasure every touch, every kiss, every tug on our hearts?

How many people experience a love that had no beginning and no end? It always existed. It always will. It was pure and unselfish. It couldn't be diminished nor tarnished by time or circumstance.

Do I not still hear the sweetness lifting off your every word?

I see your wedding dress in our closet. We didn't quite make it, did we? But if the true meaning of marriage is for two to become one, we were wed long ago.

I walk to your birdfeeder every morning and try in vain to greet your friends. Their song is sad.

I turn the corner and breathe your scent. I look, but do not see you. Still you linger.

I pick up my pen to write, but have no reason. I have shared life with you. I am complete.

I lie in our mountain of leaves and gaze into the sky. I see your face. I was wrong about the sun. You did not reflect its light. It borrows its light from you.

I did not want the best years of your life. I wanted you, Anna.

You are mine. And I am yours. I am content.

Lonely. Aching. Broken. But content.

Kirk Martin

I waited a lifetime for this brief moment. It will not be so long until we shall be together again.

I pray you are the angel God sends for me.

The heavens are brighter now with you there.

But I miss you here, Anna.

Epilogue

HE LAID his pen down on pages still wet with black ink, and buried his face in his hands. Hands whose lines could tell but one story, hands that had penned words that only she understood. Rising slowly from the leather chair, he leaned over the desk and blew out the flickering candle. He walked by the stray light of the moon from the den to the family room, grabbing the old white sweater tossed across the back of the sofa.

The screen door creaked slowly and slammed behind him. He shuffled across the clapboard porch and fell into his rocking chair. He looked at the empty chair beside him and ached.

Evan whispered Anna's name into the night sky and reached for her hand.

A NEW DIRECTION

EARLIER DETECTION

Friends...You Can
Count On

Currently more than one million women are unaware that a deadly cancer is growing inside their bodies. Diligent monthly self-exams, yearly doctor's exams and even annual mammograms might not detect breast cancer until it has been present for 5-8 years.

I am honored to partner with *Friends...You Can Count On,* the nation's only non-profit organization dedicated solely to discovering earlier methods of detection. *Friends* foresees the day when a simple and reliable lab test will detect breast cancer before a tumor has formed.

$1 from the purchase price of this novel will be donated to fund research designed to achieve this critical goal. To find out more about how you can help, please contact *Friends*:

1-888-792-3062
www.earlier.org

www.shadeofthemaple.com

Thank you for purchasing *Shade of the Maple*. I welcome your comments and invite you to visit my web site.

Kirk Martin